NERD RAGE UPRISING

STEVE WOLLETT

Dedicated to all of the Nerds in my life from my gaming friends to my convention friends. You people inspire me and through that inspiration, make me strive to be a better person.

ACKNOWLEDGMENTS

Friends and family have supported me throughout my career. Making movies, publishing books and game, and even my songwriting. Throughout my life I have been fortunate and privileged enough to always have a support system. It was this support system of loving devotion that has enabled me to succeed in life. For this I am most grateful to my fans, my friends, and mostly my wife. Without that support this book would not even be a blip on the radar of my mind.

Nerd Rage Uprising

The Game

Download for Android

Download for iOS

Steve Wollett

Introduction

Being a nerd is not always easy. There are times when the world around you seems to be dancing to its own tune and you are on the outside, unable to understand. Sometimes, you are the life of a party because of your vast and unconventional displays of knowledge. At other times, you are the outsider, the arrogant ass who is making a fool of himself, simply by trying to share some tidbit of trivia that excites you. The problem often is, that you take pleasure from things that seem inconceivable to the general masses. Unfortunately, when you get excited by an Easter egg discovered in a video game or book, everyone else just thinks you are a buffoon. Or worse, when you demonstrate your vast knowledge of the workings of the legal system of Hammurabi, your family thinks that you are trying to make them all look stupid. Being a nerd is hard work. Unfortunately, this work is rarely respected. Luckily for us nerds, we are a tribal bunch and our time seems to be on the rise. Maybe the next decade will prove to be the decade of the nerd. It certainly appears that being a nerd is more popular today than ever before.

Steve Wollett

Chapter 1

The sound of a running engine gave off the illusion that the dark forest was lively. The trees were dark brown, almost black, and their leaves were a dull green color that made them look even creepier. A strong gust of wind shattered the omnipresent yet unmoving painting the forest it had created, and for the first time since the long trip there was movement around. No longer did the young girl in the car feel like she was stuck in an endless loop of a rocky path leading to nowhere. Soft hands were placed against the cool window, bright eyes curiously glancing around and searching for something interesting. There was a phone next to her – its tiny blue light had turned red, signifying that it had no battery. The device was placed on top of a black leather school bag with a small golden badge on the side. The badge showed the name of the school the girl was going to start going to – St Ambrose. A tired sigh escaped the girl's lips and she almost dozed off until she heard her name.

"Eiko, sweetie, we're here." A feminine voice spoke out. The woman, Eiko's mother, craned her neck to the side so that she could look at her. Thin crimson lips were pursed in an excited smile – the expression made the girl look forward to starting school again. The sounds of the car slowly faded away and Eiko saw the dead trees stop moving.

The girl ran a hand over her face as if it would help her fight off the evident exhaustion from the long car ride and shifted away from the window. "Finally," she grumbled out, "I thought we'd be stuck on the road forever."

"Nonsense, darling." The woman quietly chuckled before opening the door. Her heels clicked against the hard ground as she made her way to the back of the car in order to pull out her daughter's suitcase. It wasn't anything special, except for the multiple Call of the Warrior and Castles and Drakes stickers. Eiko was a *bit* of a gamer. "I can't believe my little girl is all grown up now…" The mother continued, voice shaky and much weaker than before. Her thin and bony fingers were tightly clutching the suitcase's handle until Eiko got closer. The woman suddenly dropped the item and swiftly wrapped her arms around the girl, trapping her in a tight hug.

Eiko was taken aback at first and didn't know how to react. *If this was in a video game, it'd definitely be a quick time event*, she thought to herself. Nonetheless, she hugged her mother back and the moment she felt the oxygen leave her lungs, she pushed the woman away. "It's going to be fine, Mom, sheesh," she sighed, "growing up is a part of life. I'm level twelve now and I feel pretty good about it."

The mother extended an arm and gave her a gentle pat on the head. "I know you'll be fine dear, I'll just miss you a lot. Be sure to call me at least once a day, alright? Promise?"

Eiko mentally rolled her eyes at the dramatic display of affection and tightened the pink bow holding her hair. "I will, I will, as long as I don't forget to charge my phone." She mumbled out and reached for the suitcase with her free hand. Both bags weren't as heavy as she expected but, then again, Eiko had completely forgotten about the fact that they were supposed to leave today and had a hard time packing after a long night of mindless gaming. She knew she had taken everything important, though – tabletop games and her phone. As long as there were computers in the school, she was sure she'd have a wonderful time no matter what happened.

After waving goodbye to her mother and escaping before the woman could trap her in her tight grasp once again, Eiko half-jogged up to the gates of the school. She held the suitcase with her right hand, whereas her left was clutching the school bag and phone. When she glanced up, she felt taken aback by the iron gate; it consisted of tall thin poles and had the school's name written on the top in golden letters, similar to the badge on her bag. *This certainly isn't creepy at all*, Eiko sarcastically thought to herself, taking a small step closer. She stood on her toes in order to look behind it, searching for anyone that would open the gate for her. *Isn't this supposed to be the first day of school? Don't tell me I'm about to play a single-player campaign.*

As if her thoughts had been heard, there was suddenly a loud creak as the iron bars started slowly moving to the side. The sound made her physically cringe – it was just like chalk on a blackboard. The girl felt a wave of relief wash over her and her shoulders slouched, posture now relaxed even if her eyes kept looking around. There still wasn't anyone there even after she got inside, hands tightly clutching her bags. She usually wasn't the type to get scared but the whole school building looked like it had come out of a horror game. There wasn't anything else left to do other than head straight to the vast building that resembled a castle more than a school. It definitely did look interesting even if the atmosphere around it was dark. The moment Eiko walked up to the two tall doors that were painted a crimson red, she heard a voice call out in the distance. The girl stiffened and her fight or flight reflexes kicked in until she saw a young woman lightly jog up to her. When she got close enough to the girl, she stopped in her tracks and placed her hands on her thighs in order to catch her breath.

It was a nun.

There was awkward silence and Eiko could only give her a skeptical stare, one brow raised in confusion and lips pursed in a thoughtful frown. Less than a minute later, though, the woman stood up and arched her back. "Welcome to St Ambrose School!" She happily chirped, even if her smile looked fake and didn't reach her eyes. The woman looked much younger than what Eiko had expected and the fact that she had a white wimple with a black veil and a black dress made her look more like she had come out of a history book. Then again... Eiko had never met a nun in real life before. "I apologize for being late. I am Sister Ann and I was given the task to help you feel at home at St Ambrose. Follow me, please, I will show you where the dorms are located."

"Okay," Eiko mumbled out, tilting her head to the side. She stood completely still for a few moments, watching the way the black veil flew in the air when a gust of wind passed by. It was chilly – the weather was surprisingly much colder than what she had expected. She knew that the school's location was deep inside a thick forest, although the lack of sunlight was suspicious. The two females walked in silence in the complete opposite direction of the wide building with the red doors. The floor was made out of dull gray concrete and there were dark leaves everywhere that crunched beneath Eiko's shoes, the sound of which was satisfying.

"We're here," Sister Ann quietly spoke. Her shoes clicked against the concrete, although they weren't nearly as loud as the heels of Eiko's mother. She was standing in front of two vertical buildings that were almost as high as the school itself. After motioning for Eiko to follow her to the left one, she pushed the dark green iron door open. The sound was just as bad as the front gate but the girl grit her teeth and clutched the strap of her school bag. "This is the girls' dorm," the woman stated, "you'll be staying on the top floor. All the others have already been taken."

Eiko gave a shrug even if she knew that Sister Ann couldn't see it. *The less people that bother me, the better*, she thought to herself. The narrow staircase proved out to be a difficult task to complete and by the time the two girls got to the top, they were both panting. Eiko's wrists felt as if they were about to pop and the suitcase suddenly seemed much heavier than before. Her thighs were burning and she cursed herself for being so out of shape. *I need to put more points in stamina and strength, those are my weakest stats*, she mentally noted.

"This... This is your room," Sister Ann spoke between deep breaths. She pulled out a small key with the number thirteen and unlocked the door. The woman held the entrance open with her hand and moved to the side so that Eiko could enter. "Here's the key. Please, be very careful with it. There aren't any spare ones for students."

The girl nodded. "Sure, no problem." She gently grabbed the key and thanked the nun for her help.

"If you have any questions or want to report a problem, the school secretary is on the right side of the hallway in the main building." Sister Ann bowed her head and clasped her hands together. "Enjoy your stay at St Ambrose. Order is eternal."

The last part made Eiko turn around in surprise. When she was about to speak, though, the nun was already gone. She could hear the echo of her shoes sound through the narrow stairs. "Order is eternal, huh?" The girl grinned, finally making her way inside. She took off her bright pink shoes and placed her suitcase to the side. "They should see my room by the time I'm done unpacking. Chaos is eternal."

After placing her school bag onto the small bed in the corner of the room, Eiko decided to explore her new home. It was worse than she expected, much to her annoyance. The walls were supposed to be white but gave off a pastel blue hue. There was only one window in the room and it was darker than outside – Eiko wasn't tall enough to reach it, which is why she had to pull the barely standing wooden chair in order to use it as leverage to close it. The chair creaked each time she moved and shook when she first stood up. She pushed it back to the desk in the opposite corner of the room. The desk itself was, just like everything so far, extremely small. Needless to say, the air in the room was just as chilly as outside and it stayed that way long after the window was closed. There was an old heater next to the bed but Eiko decided not to use it after turning it on once – it made unearthly sounds as if it was possessed by a ghost. The bathroom wasn't anything special either; it looked like any other bathroom except smaller in size. There weren't any cooking utensils but Eiko didn't mind that since she wasn't much into cooking and didn't know how to do it either way. Even in games she never chose cooking as a profession – it was foreign and scary in her opinion.

Upon finishing the quick tour, the girl made her way back to her suitcase in the hallway. She swiftly carried it over to her bed and started rummaging through her clothes after carefully taking out her tabletop games and placing them on the desk. She made sure to plug her phone in so that it could charge, and right as she was about to open up one of her favorite dungeon crawler games, there was a siren that sound through the whole area. Eiko almost dropped the phone in surprise and her stomach twisted in anxiety.

Sirens are bad, right? What is going on? Are we under attack?

Suddenly, the creepy sound stopped. There was a raspy feminine voice that echoed throughout the air and replaced it. It definitely wasn't Sister Ann, that much Eiko was sure of. "Dinner time starts in ten minutes."

"Oh boy," Eiko spoke to herself, "I sure do love strict timing rules."

Chapter 2

Dinner time turned out to be a total mess. Eiko tried not to think too much about it, although her mind was evil and kept bringing her back to all the embarrassing moments. It was barely 9pm but all the students were made to go back to their dorms and head straight to bed – it wasn't that surprisingly considering the fact that class started at 6am each day. Eiko was completely shocked upon realizing that and almost forgot about her making a fool out of herself; her mind was far too occupied with the horror of lack of sleep. *No living breathing human being should get up so early*, Eiko mentally whined, eyes firmly set onto the ground. There were different students that passed by but thankfully they fully ignored her existence – this was something she was used to since primary school. Then again, she was sure she stuck out compared to the others due to her bright clothes. She was wearing a pastel pink T-shirt, along with denim shorts and sneakers. That wasn't so bad, right? Unfortunately, the school's uniform consisted of dull gray clothes that matched the dark exterior of the campus. She stuck out like a toxic animal in a jungle.

"Did you get yelled at 'cus of your clothes?" A male voice could be heard behind her. Eiko instantly stiffened and straightened her back, turning around so quickly that her neck popped. She thought it was a priest or nun that were about to scold her even further and pour salt in her wound. Upon seeing that it was just another normal student, though, her shoulders instantly slouched in relief. It was a boy around her age, wearing similar glasses – he didn't look anything special but at least he was wearing the school's uniform, unlike her.

Eiko sighed, "Yup. Wouldn't recommend it."

"You'll get over it soon enough, trust me." The stranger smiled. "I don't know if it'll make you feel better but the same thing happened to me yesterday. It's definitely not the best feeling."

The girl raised a brow in suspicion before looking the boy up and down. "… Are you new?" She cautiously asked.

"Yeah," he sighed, "unfortunately. The name's Dexter, by the way."

She returned the kind smile and extended her arm for a handshake. It was nice to meet someone who was new and most likely just as miserable as her. "I'm Eiko."

Dexter firmly shook her hand and let it go before speaking once again. "Did you move in the dorms yet?" He took a step closer and motioned for her to continue walking so that they wouldn't be in the middle of the courtyard.

"Dorms? More like prison cells." Eiko rolled her eyes. "Yup, I did. My room needs a *lot* of decorating, though." Even if she disliked small talk, the conversation she was having put her mind and body at ease.

Dexter chuckled, "Same here, same here. Well, at least we aren't forced to sleep outside. I was pretty sure I would be when I first showed up."

"There's no way." Eiko giggled, covering her mouth with her free hand. "That'd be too much even for this school. Why are you here anyway?"

The boy sighed. There was heavy silence for a moment as they both made their way to the boys' dorm. He sat on the bench on the side of the entrance and placed his school bag on the ground. "It's not anything special or interesting," he noted, "it's just that my parents are super busy since they travel a lot. I guess they searched for a boarding school and, voila, this is what they found." Dexter folded his arms across his chest, lips forming a childish pout. "Yay, this is a nice school that *totally* cares about its students," he sarcastically spoke.

Yikes, he certainly doesn't like this place, Eiko mentally spoke, sitting on the boy's left side. She put her school bag over her thighs. "It could always be worse." She shrugged, despite her statement sounding more like a question rather than confirmation.

"They took my bowties, man." Dexter leaned his head against the cold concrete wall of the building. "My bowties!" He repeated with a raised voice, hands motioning upwards in order to show his disdain. "They told me they weren't allowed. Why? What have they done?"

Eiko couldn't help but raise a brow. Dexter certainly didn't seem like the type of person to even be interested in formal clothing, though she supposed she shouldn't judge people based on their appearance, especially since she didn't know anything about him. Then again, his obsessions with bowties was concerning. "I mean... Maybe they had to deal with a powerful bowtie boss that almost destroyed the school."

"Bowtie boss?" Now was Dexter's turn to look at her in confusion. "A boss fight?"

The girl defensively raised her hands. "I—It's just an idea."

"So you play video games, huh?" The boy thoughtfully hummed, putting his hand on his chin. "That's pretty cool."

Eiko's face instantly flushed in embarrassment. She kept forgetting that most people considered gamers to be lame nerds who didn't have social lives. *Damn it, I ruined my chance to be cool,* she whined. "I only play sometimes, you know? I'm definitely not obsessed or anything." She nervously laughed.

Dexter shook his head. "Sure, I believe you." He teased her, sticking his tongue out. "Don't worry. I like video games – I don't play them that often since I like other things, but I don't mind gamers."

Eiko sighed in relief. "I almost thought I ruined everything," she mumbled out, letting out a long sigh of relief. Thankfully, it only took her a few moments to get ahold of herself. "What do you like?" She leaned forwards, glancing up at Dexter's face. It was only fair, in her opinion, to know something embarrassing that they boy enjoyed.

Now was Dexter's turn to blush in embarrassment. Every time he told a girl about his interests, they always mockingly laughed at him. "Comics are cool, I guess." He looked away in a vain attempt to hide his face. "Cosplay too – stuff like that."

"Cosplay?!" Eiko raised her voice, instantly leaning in forwards. She wasn't too big on comic books, but she definitely was a fan of dressing up as different characters from her video and tabletop games. "I love watching those types of shows. Some people are so talented, it's unreal."

Dexter perked up and glanced around in paranoia. There was a group of male students who were heading towards the boys' dorms. Their pace was extremely slow since they were mostly talking with each other. "Shush." He brought his index finger to his lips. "Don't let the others hear."

"Why?" Eiko tilted her head to the side.

The boy sighed, "The same reason you got embarrassed when your video game addiction was exposed."

"It's not an addiction!" The girl tried to defend herself, even if she was an extremely bad liar. "Okay, maybe a little bit…" Her voice trailed off. Without thinking too much about it, she pulled out her phone out of the front pocket of her school bag and instantly opened up one of the apps after entering her password. She tapped on a bright yellow icon in the corner of the screen that completely went dark for a few seconds before the logo of the game 'Killer Dungeon' showed up. "Look at this," she started, going through the slides that showed up, "how can you *not* be addicted to such a good game? Have you played it?"

As much as Dexter wanted to pay attention to the phone screen, he couldn't tear his gaze away from the group of boys that were only getting closer by the moment. "M—Maybe we should check it out later," he quietly spoke, reaching for his school bag. Despite Eiko not knowing anything about the students at St Ambrose, Dexter was well aware of the notorious bullies that existed everywhere.

Unfortunately, the girl was too busy fixing up her team for the upcoming dungeon crawler event. Her eyes were glued to the bright screen – it was as if the world had stopped moving around her. She didn't hear Dexter's worried pleas for them to go back to their dorms, nor did she realize that one of the boys had made his way in front of her. The ignorance lasted up until she felt rough hands reach for her phone in order to successfully pry it out of her hands. Eiko was completely taken by surprise – at first she thought it was one of the nuns who were keeping watch, though as she glanced up with a glare, she saw that it was someone she hadn't seen before.

The boy was tall, much taller and wider than Dexter. He looked like the typical jock and the girl couldn't hide her confusion at first. Considering how stuck up the school itself was, she didn't think she would see any sporty type of people out and about in such a conservative place. The stranger had black hair that was slicked back with hair gel and bright blue eyes that contrasted his tan skin. His thin lips were pursed in a wicked grin that almost fully made them disappear and he had extended one of his hands high up in the air, firmly holding the phone.

Eiko furrowed her brows in frustration and stood up. "Give it back," she spoke, trying to reach for it with her own arm. Unfortunately, she wasn't even close. "It's mine."

"Y'know, it's been a while since I've had a phone," the boy ly spoke as if they were having a normal conversation as friends. "Yours looks pretty nice too. One of the newer models, I presume?"

"Give it back." Eiko raised her voice, glaring daggers into his twisted face. She stood on her toes and lightly jumped but the bully moved his hand away in order to prevent her from getting the device.

He laughed in her face. "Or else what? Lil' Miss Colorful is gonna go tell a teacher? You do know what's gonna happen if they find out, right? It'll be bye-bye phone."

Eiko's expression turned from anger to confusion and disbelief. She quickly glanced over to her side in order to look at Dexter whose face had paled. He gave her a nod that confirmed what the bully had said. The girl let out a sigh of frustration and sat down with such force that she shook the whole bench. She folded her arms across her chest. "What do you want from me?"

"Are you really that stupid?" The boy shook his head. "I want your phone, duh." He held the device in front of her face in order to taunt her. This time, though, Eiko managed to keep her cool even if her stomach was burning from anger and her face was red from the frustration she felt. "Unless you want to lose your phone 'till summer vacation, you'll lend it to me. That's what friends are for, right?"

"Come on, man, leave her alone." Dexter finally spoke up, even if his voice was shaky.

The bully laughed even louder – his voice echoed throughout the area. "Look who decided to speak up! I thought the cat got your tongue, Dexter," he mockingly said. "Now, unless you want the same thing from yesterday to happen to you again, you'll keep your mouth shut. That way no one gets hurt, alright?"

Eiko kept glancing between Dexter and bully, face worried and anxious. "I'll just head back to my dorm," she quietly spoke, grabbing her school bag as she stood up. She knew that no matter what she said or did it would make things worse and even if Dexter didn't do anything to help her, she still didn't want him to get hurt.

The girl thought that it wouldn't get worse than the first day of school but she certainly was wrong.

Chapter 3

Eiko plopped face first into the soft sheets of the narrow bed in the small room. She didn't bother taking off her shoes – she was completely done with St Ambrose and its students, and the fact that it was only the beginning made her fume from rage. She pushed herself up in order to grab the pillow and covered her face with it, screaming with all her might. The sound was muffled and when she was done, she turned on her back and stared up at the ceiling with unfocused eyes. The corners of her eyes stung from the tears that were threatening to fall but she kept taking deep breaths in order to calm herself down. After wiping her eyes with her forearm, she pushed herself up into a sitting position and glanced to the nearby suitcase. The stickers served as a reminder of her past life and she couldn't help but glare at them as she made her way to the case. Eiko sat on the floor and opened the zipper, the sound of which was the only thing that could be heard in the deathly silence. It was now fully dark; there weren't any birds or students outside and even if people had conversations in front of the dorms, the girl wouldn't be able to hear them due to being so high up.

"I got scolded because of this ugly thing?" Eiko mumbled out to herself before pulling out the dull gray school uniform. She held it in front of her face for a few moments, carefully inspecting the details (or lack thereof). "At least the pink parts go well with my bow," she sighed, one hand ly reaching for the back of her head. She pulled the bow and let her hair fall loose. Even if the feeling of relief was welcome, the frustration deep down inside was far from disappearing. Eiko put down the uniform, gaze moving towards the high yet small window on the side of her bed. The leaves of one of the taller trees could be seen as if it was a shadow of a monster looming in. The girl shook her head and stood up from the floor, pushing her suitcase and the uniform on top of it to the side with her foot.

As Eiko made her way to the desk, she noticed the round alarm clock in the corner of it. She hadn't seen it before, surprisingly. Bright eyes narrowed down into a glare of disbelief – it was barely 9pm! There was no way she would be able to fall asleep, especially not without her phone or laptop that she had left home. She was used to heading to bed extremely late and sleeping throughout most of the day. Her sleep schedule became even worse during the summer vacation since there was no school to keep her on track. Whenever she couldn't sleep, she usually watched gameplay videos. Now? She was left to her own devices. The only type of games she had available were tabletop but those were impossible to play with one person. *Maybe Dexter would want to play with me,* she thought, glancing to the suitcase. *No,* she shook her head, *not after today. He's just like the rest of them.*

Eiko sat on the wooden chair and placed her elbow over the desk, putting her chin in the palm of her hand. "I need to get my phone back…" she quietly spoke, dragging the nails of her free hand in a circular motion. The girl's eyes were narrowed down, lips formed a frown. A tired sigh echoed throughout the mostly empty room as Eiko extended both arms over the desk and placed her forehead over them. "This is *SO* not fair."

Unfortunately for the girl, life wasn't a game. It didn't have set rules that everyone was made to follow if they didn't want to be banned. People were free to have their own personalities and treat others the way they wanted to but Eiko couldn't believe that some people chose to be mean to others out of their own free will. It just didn't make any sense. Why couldn't all the bullies mind their own business? That's what she had done throughout a bigger portion of her life and everything had been fine… Up until now.

Before Eiko knew it, she drifted off into a light sleep. She would've liked to at least use the uncomfortable looking bed but before she could gather the strength to get up from the desk, she dozed off on top of her arms. It was hard not to be sleepy without anything to do – boredom was a powerful enemy. The adrenaline from the face off with the bully had also left her body, leaving her mentally and physically exhausted.

Chapter 4

There was a loud, ear-piercing sound. It resembled a furious dragon, a demon crawling its way from the pits of hell. It was as if someone was being tortured. Eiko's whole body jumped from fear and she stood up so quickly that blood rushed to her legs and her vision became dark and blurry for a few seconds. She would have fallen down had it not been for the desk in front of her. Eiko managed to put her hands on top of it and hold her balance, although the agonizing sound was still present. Her head was starting to hurt and after maintaining her composure, she started looking around for the origin of it. Thankfully, she managed to see that it was coming from the alarm clock in front of her before she lost her mind. One hand swiftly reached in order to turn it off. The girl sat down on the chair again and as much as she wanted to hold her head with her hands, she realized that they had been asleep. The prickles of nerves were now starting to spread through her hands, leading up to her elbow and reaching all the way up to her shoulder. She had to let them hang by her sides.

That's what I get for sleeping on the desk, Eiko mentally scolded herself as she waited for the uncomfortable feeling to go away. She had enough time to stare at the clock in front. The quiet ticking of the arrows faded as quickly as it showed up each time they moved. It was as if it was mocking her. Eiko couldn't believe that it actually was 5:30am. People kept telling her that whenever she started work she'd have to get up around that time, though she was still twelve and couldn't be more bitter about the fact. *Time to be a cookie cutter student, I guess,* Eiko rolled her eyes and finally stood up from the desk. She walked over to the suitcase, ly grabbing the uniform and threw it on the bed. Half-kneeling in front of it, she rummaged through the smaller pockets and pulled out a toothbrush. Without wasting any precious time, she brushed her teeth, put her hair up with her favorite pink bow and struggled with the uniform. Despite it being very simple on the outside, the cotton material made it hard for her to throw the coat over her head. Much to Eiko's despise, she had to open up almost all of the buttons. Thankfully the shirt underneath was easily put on and the pink tie was skillfully turned into a bow. The only things that were left were the dull red stockings and matching shoes. After Eiko was done putting on the school uniform, she walked up to the horizontal mirror in the bathroom and painfully twisted her body in order to take a look at every bit. "If only I had my phone," she sighed, "whatever. I'll get it today." The girl took a deep breath and curled her lips into a fake smile as she straightened her back. Her parents had told her to be the best student she could, although she was sure that no matter how hard she tried, she wouldn't be able to impress the sadistic priests and nuns. Eiko grabbed her school bag, slung it over her shoulder and after making sure the door for her room was locked, she started going down the stairs.

The girl's gaze was firmly locked onto her feet because she was afraid that one wrong move would end with her falling and possibly breaking something. She wasn't a big fan of the shoes – they were uncomfortable around the sides of her feet. Before she could mentally complain, though, she bumped into something firm. The 'something' turned out to be 'someone', much to her horror. When she glanced up, she saw the body of a blonde girl hunch over. Thankfully, due to being a gamer, Eiko's reflexes were extremely sharp. She managed to extend her arm and grabbed the stranger by the collar of her shirt. She gently pulled her up and after making sure the girl could keep her balance, she defensively raised her hands in front of herself. "I— I'm so sorry!" Eiko exclaimed. "Are you hurt?"

It felt like the blonde was turning around in slow motion. The girl's stomach twisted in anxiety during that time – the last thing Eiko wanted to do was cause trouble for her neighbors. When she could finally see her face, the gamer's mouth opened in amazement. Before her was one of the most beautiful girls she had ever seen. Her long black lashes almost fully concealed her eyes whenever she blinked. Her silky long hair flew behind her as she moved and the side of her bangs was held up with a pink flower-shaped pin. Unlike Eiko, the first three buttons of her shirt were open, exposing thin collarbones and pale skin.

She'd definitely be an elf, Eiko thought, *but I don't know what class. Maybe a Mage? She doesn't seem like the melee type. Maybe a Cleric!*

"Uh, hello?" The stranger raised a brow, waving her hand in front of the gamer's face in order to make her snap out of her thoughts.

Eiko blushed upon realizing she had spaced off. "I'm sorry!" She repeated. "I—I wasn't looking where I was going. I promise I'll be more careful."

"Promises aren't going to fix my undershirt." The blonde rolled her eyes. "You know there aren't any spare official clothes, right?"

The girl's face paled in horror. "… I don't know how to sew. I'm really, really, *really* sorry." An idea sprung into Eiko's mind. She started taking off her coat. "Here, you can have mine."

"Ew, gross." The blonde backed away. "Are you crazy?"

"Kate!" A high-pitched voice screamed from the

entrance. "Where are you? We're going to be, like, totally late for class. If you take more than ten more seconds we're leaving. C'mon, Slowpoke!"

The blonde girl, Kate, stiffened up and looked behind her as if she was expecting someone to show up. Upon glancing back to Eiko, she shook her head and held her hand in front of her face again. "See you never, weirdo." She chuckled, finally heading down the stairs.

So much for making a good impression, Eiko sighed. This time her shoulders were slouched in shame and her pace was slow. She didn't care about being late to class – her day couldn't get any more horrible. The first class was supposed to be History; she didn't even care about the subject. The only type of history she was interested in was the lore of the different universes in games. Everything else was lame and boring in her opinion. It's not like she had much of a choice, unfortunately.

Upon heading to the main entrance of the vast school building, Eiko felt the aura of intimidation get to her. It looked like a castle, except that it wasn't the type of castle you'd see in a fairytale. It was more of an abandoned and haunted location. After taking a deep breath, the girl slowly pushed open one of the doors in order to slither inside. Despite the school's outside walls being dark, the interior was the complete opposite. Everything was white, except for the dark gray lockers and the wooden floor that creaked each time someone stepped on it. The school hallway was tall and wide but all the students still pushed each other in order to get through. The realization that Eiko didn't know what her locker was suddenly dawned upon her and she felt herself at a loss of what to do. Halfway through mentally battling with her desire to head back to her dorm and never come out, she felt a hand on her shoulder. The girl instantly jumped in surprise and spun around, holding her fists in front of her and the culprit. She was ready to fight if it was her bully. Surprisingly enough – it wasn't.

Dexter took a big step back in order to avoid the upcoming blow. "H—Hey, it's me! Dexter! We met yesterday," he defensively spoke.

Even if Eiko relaxed her fists and her posture wasn't in a battle stance anymore, she still glared up at the boy. It'd be a while before she would be able to forget his lack of action when it came down to dealing with the bully. "What do you want?" she roughly asked, "Class is starting soon."

"I'm sorry about yesterday," Dexter sighed, shoulders slouching in defeat. "But—" He perked up with a smile. "I've got a plan."

"A plan for what?" Eiko raised a brow and motioned for him to follow her to the side so that they weren't an obstacle in the middle of the school hallway. She leaned against one of the many white walls and folded her arms across her chest, glancing up in expectation.

Dexter's innocent smile turned into an evil smirk. "I found out where Christian's room is." He clasped his hands together.

"Christian?" Eiko hummed. "Don't think I know anyone with that name, sorry."

The boy sighed, lowering his voice. "Oh, come on! You know Christian, the big evil bully dude. The guy who took your phone, remember?"

Eiko felt as if she had been kicked in the stomach. She gulped before speaking. "Yeah... I remember him alright." She glanced away with a glare. "I also remember *you* not helping me."

"I told you, I'm sorry about that. I'm just—" Dexter awkwardly motioned with his hands. "—Not good when it comes to dealing with bullies. I did risk my skin in order to find his room, though."

The girl huffed. "So what? There's no way he'll voluntarily give us his key and there aren't any spares. Didn't Sister Ann tell you?"

"What? No, no, that's a lie." Dexter pushed his glasses up the bright of his nose with his index finger. "Listen, there aren't any spares when it comes down to *student* keys but if we managed to snatch it from a staff member, we'll be able to enter."

Eiko almost laughed at his proposal – she barely managed to control herself. After all, it was Dexter, of all people, who was suddenly acting brave. She didn't know much about him but that didn't change the fact that he had showed his evident cowardice. "This doesn't sound like you at all. Are you sure you didn't hit your head on the way here?" Eiko smirked.

The boy's smile instantly turned into a frown. "I've been here for less than a week and I'm dying of boredom. If I help you get your phone back, I'll expect payment," he noted, "such as me playing the games on it."

"Is it really that bad?" Eiko's smirk faded away as she glanced up in disbelief.

Dexter's expression was dead serious. "They stole all my comic books the moment they found out about them. Guess who told the Principal about them?"

"Christian," Eiko hissed.

The boy nodded. "This is why we need to get your phone back ASAP before he gives it to one of the nuns."

"Why would he do that?" The girl's brows furrowed in worry. "What even is he winning from this? Doesn't he like to have fun?"

"That's his way of having fun," Dexter mumbled out, glancing at the ground in sadness.

Suddenly, the loud school bell took the duo out of their thoughts. They both stiffened up as if they had been caught making an evil masterplan. When Eiko looked behind the boy, she saw that the school hallway was almost empty, except for the few students who were tightly clutching their bags and running towards their class. "W—We gotta go ASAP," she firmly stated, "but, ugh, I don't even know where my locker is!"

"The number on your key is the same as your locker. They both use one key." Dexter quickly spoke from the distance, already heading to his room.

"Thanks." Eiko raised her arm in order to give him a wave before hurrying up herself. She didn't have time to put all the unneeded items in her locker, though it was good to know she had one. Eiko half-jogged up to each room, trying to search the cursed letter 'H' for History. By the time she got to the end of the hallway she saw that the door on the right had what she was looking for. The school hallway was extremely quiet and empty. Eiko's stomach twisted in anxiety and she took a deep breath, one shaky hand reaching for the handle. The door loudly creaked, alerting everyone present of her arrival.

The room was much smaller than the hallway. The walls were the same color as the ones outside and the floor, desks and chairs were made out of wood. There were four lines of desks that were connected to one another. The wide blackboard in the middle of the room was already full of white chalk despite class having started a minute ago. There were a few windows on the right side of the room, opposite of Eiko's location. All of them were open and the room was the same temperature as outside – far too cold for the girl to be comfortable.

Eiko slowly closed the door behind her and bowed her head. "I apologize for being late. I got lost on my way here b—but I managed to find the room."

The teacher, who was a much older nun than the one who had helped Eiko out in the beginning craned her neck. Her dull blue eyes were hidden behind the horrifying amount of wrinkles across her face. She was chubby and was already carrying a glare across her deathly features. Eiko would later find out that her name was Sister Mary Bernadette. Without saying anything, the old woman stood up from the desk and the loud pop form her knees could be heard by all the students. She threateningly made her way to the girl, each step shaking the podium in front of the blackboard. Even if the gamer stood completely unmoving, she was panicking inside. Her whole body told her to run but she knew it was too late – there was no escape. She was trapped between the door and the teacher.

The nun extended her arm towards Eiko who could only stare at her in confusion. Thankfully, it didn't take her long to realize what was needed of her. Without thinking too much about it, the girl extended her hands forwards. The next thing Eiko heard was a loud sound as agonizing pain spread across her body. Her vision became darker for a moment until her brain found out what was going on. The teacher had slapped her hands with a long wooden ruler as punishment.

Eiko jumped away when she got hit. Her back hit the door and she gasped in pain before biting the inside of her cheek in order to keep herself from screaming from the pain. It was awful. Eiko's heart beat rapidly against her ribcage as if it was trying to escape. She could feel cold sweat beads form across her forehead and neck. The only thing that took her out of her painful trance was the quiet whisper that gently grazed her ears. Eiko cautiously glanced to the owner, trying to figure out the words.

A girl at the first desk had leaned forwards, covering the side of her mouth. "You need to sit down. Do it, quick," she quietly commanded.

The gamer blinked once, then twice in confusion. When she looked in front of her again, she saw that the nun had sat back down on the desk and was continuing with her lesson. Eiko glanced at the girl and mouthed a 'thanks' before cautiously making her way to the side in order to sit on the furthest desk. She couldn't even hear what she lesson was about – her ears were loudly ringing and whenever she looked at her hands and saw the bright red line that was further spreading to the sides of her skin, she cringed. Even if the pain faded away by the end of the lesson, Eiko was still afraid to properly hold a pen. This is why she feigned writing and prayed that the teacher wouldn't stand up in order to see whether everyone was working

Eiko couldn't believe she made it until the end of the class. The moment the bell rang, she felt a huge wave of relief wash over her and she almost fell over the desk in her attempt to get out of the cursed room as quickly as she could. She couldn't imagine the fact that she'd have to take History three time a week. Bright eyes cautiously glanced around, searching for a familiar face in the crowds of people swarming around the lockers. When she didn't see Dexter, she carefully made her way to her locker. Eiko half-closed her eyes, expecting something to jump out of it when it got opened. *No jump scares... yet*, she mentally complained before placing the big history book inside. Eiko closed the locker and made sure to lock it. Her next class was Math but she still had some time left. The best course of action would be to wait for Dexter to show up, that much she was sure of, which is why she leaned against the cold locker and kept her arms behind her in order to hide her bruise. The last thing she wanted was to be made fun of for being a troublemaker.

The gamer didn't know how much time had passed until she saw Dexter's face in the distance. He waved at her and she politely waved back, expecting him to head over to her location. Unfortunately, Christian showed up behind Dexter. He roughly placed his arm around the boy's neck and spoke to him, though Eiko was too far to hear what was going on. Just as she was about to head over to help her friend, the school bell rang. "Damn it," she cursed underneath her breath. When she glanced to Dexter, he motioned for her to leave. As much as Eiko wanted to help him and prove herself out to be much kinder than him when it came to dealing with bullies, the top of her arms pulsated with pain. She didn't want to get punished again. She had to do everything to avoid the horrible pain. Just thinking about it made her relive the entire situation. The girl roughly shook her head as if it would help get rid of the agonizing thoughts and practically sprinted until she reached the math room.

Unlike History, Math turned out to be as boring as possible. There was no fear lingering in the air and Eiko didn't get punished since she got into the room seconds before the teacher. The nun was thin and tall – her cheekbones were well-formed and her thin lips were always in a frown. She introduced herself in the beginning off the class; her name was Sister Helen Marie. Unfortunately, her voice was extremely quiet, it was as if she was whispering, afraid that someone would hear even if that was the point of being a teacher. Eiko had managed to snatch one of the seats in the back and was already regretting her choice. This time, though, she took notes. The nun's handwriting was the opposite of her voice – the numbers and words were big and easy to distinguish. Eiko couldn't believe that she ended up enjoying *Math*, of all the possible subjects.

As much as she tried to pay attention, her mind kept lingering to Christian and Dexter. She remembered the way Dexter motioned for her to leave him alone but… Eiko bit her bottom lip. *I shouldn't have done that,* she glanced down to her notebook in shame, *I should've helped him.* She gave out a sigh of exhaustion the moment the school bell rang and didn't waste any time getting out of the classroom. When she got to the school hallway, she started asking around the other students about Dexter. The more moments that passed without her seeing him, the more worried she got. Eiko's brows were furrowed in frustration as she went through each and every room on the bottom floor of the building in search of her friend. It wasn't until she bumped into someone that she realized she should've been more careful. *I really need to work on my coordination,* Eiko thought, finally glancing up with the intention of repeating 'sorry' until the person wasn't mad anymore. She prayed that it wouldn't be Kate again.

It definitely wasn't Kate.

In fact, it was someone much worse.

"Oh, hey there, Eiko." Christian grinned. "Fancy meetin' you here."

The girl's face paled in fear. "Wh—Where's Dexter?" She tried to sound as firm as possible, even if she knew she had failed. Her voice was shaky and weak. "Wait, how do you know my name?"

The wicked grin turned even wider as the boy breathlessly chuckled, folding his arms across his chest. "Your *friend* Dexter was nice enough to share some details 'bout you. You don't look like the gamer type." He leaned in closer. "I bet you miss your phone, huh?"

Eiko's eyes dangerously narrowed down into a glare and she grit her teeth. As much as she wanted to stand her ground, she found herself taking a small step back. "You can have my phone, I don't care*." It's not like you're going to guess the password,* she thought. "Just… stop hurting Dexter."

"Aw, does Eiko have a crush on that nerd?" Christian's grin disappeared. He looked even scarier than before.

She defensively raised her hands. "Ew, no," she said, "he's my only friend."

"Maybe if you didn't hang out with a loser like him, you'd have more than one friend." Christian rolled his eyes, no longer dangerously leaning in close. "Say, why don't you join my friends and I. We're all nice, I swear."

Are you kidding me? You stole my phone and now you want us to be friends? Is this some sort of prank? Eiko couldn't believe what she was hearing. "I'll pass." She moved to the side. "Thanks for the offer, I guess?"

Just as she about to start running, she felt a rough hand grab her by the shoulder. She squeaked in surprise and the moment panic set in her body, she heard high-pitched voices in the distance coming closer.

"Oh my gosh, is that her?"

"Wow, she looks homeless."

"I know right? She touched me. So gross."

Eiko glanced back in horror to see Kate and two other girls walk towards her. Their hair shone bright underneath the white lights in the hallway. Despite them wearing the school's uniforms, they had colorful pins and stickers that made them look unique. *I must be playing the worst possible route*, Eiko thought, *I wish I could restart.* Being bullied by four people wasn't what she had planned for the first day of school but there wasn't much she could do about it. Much to her surprise, though, things went a bit different than what she imagined.

"Ew, Christian is here too." Kate grimaced.

The boy let go of Eiko and took a step closer to the blonde. He was a head taller than her but she glared up at him, unmoving from her position. Eiko could only stare in shock at the unfolding scene. "What do you want, Kate?"

"Just wondering why you still haven't been expelled." Kate's grimace turned into a smirk. "Didn't you fail every exam last year?"

Christian grit his teeth. "It's none of your business. You almost got expelled when you showed up in heels."

"And now you're trying to drag poor old new girl down. You're evil, Chris," Kate dangerously spoke, giving out a quiet giggle. She completely ignored what the boy was saying. Instead of giving him more attention, she stepped to the side and made her way to Eiko. "Poor new girl~" she teased, sticking her tongue out.

"The 'new girl' has a name." The gamer finally took part in the conversation, voice low and annoyed. "It's Eiko."

Kate gave out a dramatic gasp. "She can say something other than 'I'm sorry'. Wow! I totally didn't expect this."

"Leave her alone, Kate, unless you wanna get hurt." Christian commanded.

The blonde swung her hips as she made her way

back to the two friends. "Haven't seen you get so defensive, Chris. Don't tell me you like her?"

"At least she doesn't need tons of makeup to look cute," he sighed, "come on, Kate. I think your eyeshadow is smeared. You better go fix it."

"First of all, rude. Second of all, I look much better than her. She's just a stupid—"

Eiko didn't hear the rest of the conversation. She managed to use the little window given to her in order to escape. She clutched her bag close to her body and sprinted for her life, dodging each student she passed by. She needed to get away from Christian and Kate – she didn't know what was going on and frankly, she didn't want to. Eiko just needed to get back to her dorm, take a breather and then continue with her search for Dexter. Unfortunately, her plan was changed once again when she saw her friend heading back to his room.

"Dexter!" She yelled out, frantically waving her arm around.

The boy was startled at first. His whole body stiffened and he quickly glanced behind his back as if he was expecting to be attacked. There was a small purple bruise on the right side of his eye, blending into his cheek. Eiko barely managed to stop herself and grabbed him by the shoulders, lightly shaking him. She was heavily panting from the jog.

"I—I don't know what's going on!" She yelled out. "The bullies are bullying each other and I barely managed to escape! Oh god, I've been looking for you *all* day. Where have you been? Wait, what happened to your cheek?"

Dexter looked completely taken aback. "Calm down, Eiko," he mumbled out, defensively raising his hands. "Take deep breaths." He motioned for his chest. "In and out, in and out."

She gave a firm nod and took a step backwards. It took her a few moments for her rapid heartbeat to calm down. The feeling that she was about to die any moment faded away and the strength needed to speak came back. Thankfully, Dexter was kind enough to wait for her. "Okay, so…" Eiko took a deep breath. "I still don't know what's going on but Christian is acting weird. We need to get my phone back ASAP." She breathed out. "Oh yeah, your cheek!"

"This?" Dexter's hand reached for the bruise. He slightly flinched upon touching it. "It's nothing. I just ran into a wall."

Eiko's expression fully showed her disbelief. She knew that Christian was the owner of the bruise.

"Do you want to go to the nurse?"

"I told you, I'm fine. It's just a little bruise – I've had much worse before. Come on, let me show you the plan I came up with." Dexter smiled.

The girl raised a brow in suspicion but followed him nonetheless. The duo made their way to the bench they had sat on the previous day. Dexter put his bag on top of it, unzipped it and pulled out a creased piece of paper. It took him a few moments to unfold it. By the time he was done, Eiko had sat on the bench.

"We have two choices." Dexter sat down next to her and placed the paper in the middle between them. "We can steal Christian's key. High risk and high reward." He lowered his voice and pointed to the left side of the paper. It showed one stick figure with question marks around its head, while two other were running away with a key. "Or…" His finger slid across the item to the right side. It showed a nun standing in front of a cupboard full of keys. "We can get the spare key from the caretaker."

Eiko sighed. "Both those plans are awful."

"I'd like to see you come up with something better." Dexter frowned.

"I would." The girl gave a shrug. "But I was trying not to get punished more than once." She held up one of her hands and faced the backside of it towards Dexter's face.

He cringed at the red line across it. "Ouch."

"Yup," Eiko grumbled out. "Okay. Let's go with the second plan."

The boy looked surprised but gave her a nod nonetheless before putting the piece of paper back into his backpack. "Didn't expect you to choose that one. Won't getting the key from Christian be much easier? I could just keep his attention."

"No way." Eiko shook her head. "I already left you alone with him once and look what happened." She pointed to his cheek. "Plus, as I said... He creeps me out."

"Alright then." Dexter rolled his shoulders. "Meet me in front of the school gates at 10pm."

Eiko's eyes widened in surprise. "That late? Our curfew's an hour earlier."

"Don't worry. Just grab your darkest clothes and we'll be able to enter the school from the gym. It's never locked and there aren't any alarms. I mean, have you seen the main building? It's ancient!" He exclaimed. "Considering how scary all the teachers are, I doubt they're worried someone might sneak in."

"Someone *dumb* enough to sneak in." Eiko corrected him, lips pursing into a smile. "I'm in. Let's do this."

The duo laughed together.

Chapter 5

Even if it wasn't the smartest plan out there, they were still excited to make it a reality. This was the most fun either of them have had since school started. Despite it being Eiko's first day, she knew it wouldn't get any better. This is why she was desperate to keep her phone safe and sound. If the nuns and priests were afraid of technology, then the device gave her even more power. It was nice to get rid of the annoying boredom too. The girl already missed her games – she had daily quests to do! After waving goodbye to her friend, she made her way back to her room. She had already forgotten about the weird territorial battle between Kate and Christian. Just as she was about to unlock her door, though, she heard the blonde's voice from the opened window on the side of the staircase. A cold shiver ran across her spine and she slammed the door shut upon entering, instantly locking it as if she in a horror game, trying to hide from a terrifying monster.

A sigh of relief escaped the girl's lips as she leaned her back against the door and relished in her freedom for a few moments. The only place where she felt safe was her room. After she calmed down, Eiko made her way over to her bed. She plopped down on it with a quiet thud and pulled her suitcase closer. *Maybe Dexter will want to play with me after we get my phone back,* she smiled, pulling out one of the two tabletop games she had carried over. Even if she still didn't know where the library was, she could only pray for it to be big enough and have enough tables for there to be room for them. Then again, that was still in the future. Eiko shook her head in order to get rid of her thoughts and placed the game on top of the desk. When she got back to her bed, she started rummaging through the case, searching for the darkest clothes she had. Even if she didn't go out often, she still liked wearing bright and colorful clothes whenever she could since she felt cute in them. Unfortunately, this meant that she didn't have a lot of dark ones. After what seemed to be hours [but was mostly minutes] Eiko managed to pull out a dark blue hoodie that belonged to her older brother. She removed the coat of the school uniform and put the clothing over the white shirt.

So far so good, she noted, *now I just need to find pants and shoes and I'll be good for tonight.* Much to her annoyance, though, she could only get her hands on a black skirt and matching platforms. Even if her legs would be exposed, she figured it was better than wearing something bright. She wasn't a big fan of tights, which is why she was pleased to remove the ones part of the uniform. Eiko pushed her glasses back into place and went to look at herself in the mirror in the bathroom. She tightened the pink bow holding a part of her hair in a loose ponytail and smiled. After spinning around a few times, the smile she carried turned into a grin.

"I look so cool!" She loudly exclaimed. "I'm like an assassin."

When she was done gushing about her looks, she made her way back to the desk. The happiness faded away the moment the girl saw that it was barely 7pm. There was still dinner time to be had. She shook her head and switched back to her school uniform in order not to further be scolded for her clothes. Even if the hours passed slowly, the excitement running through her veins was omnipresent. Eiko made sure to hide her smile when she got to the lunch hall. Her gaze was locked on the ground since she didn't want to get any unneeded attention. She didn't even see where Christian and Kate were as she walked by, swiftly going through the front tables and heading to the one in the corner after grabbing the 'mystery box' of food. That was where she met Dexter.

"You ready?" He grinned, taking a bite from his dry tuna sandwich.

Eiko gave a nod and sat down in front of him. "It's going to be so much fun!" She giggled. "I can't wait."

"That's a shame. There are two more hours left for you to wait." He shrugged.

The girl frowned. Instead of giving a response to his smug statement, she opened up the box. Inside was a simple ham sandwich that had more bread than meat. Her shoulders slouched in defeat. *I guess it's better than nothing*, she sadly thought, *it's not like they're making us pay extra for the food.*

"What'd you get?" The boy curiously asked.

Eiko removed one of the thick pieces of bread and took a glance at the interior of the sandwich with suspicion. "It's... ham, I think? I hope."

"Oh man," Dexter whined, "I got tuna. I hate fish, it's gross."

"You win some, you lose some." The girl gave a shrug and put the bread back in place. She brought the sandwich up to her face and took a bite. It wasn't good but it wasn't bad either. It didn't taste like anything, she noticed.

The rest of dinner time was spent in comfortable silence. Eiko and Dexter waited for all the other students to leave before they stood up. After all, they had inevitably become the targets of bullying. As much as the girl wanted to talk to Dexter about Kate and her vain friends, she didn't want him to do anything stupid. The less he knew about the popular girls, the better for him. He had enough to deal when it came to Christian. Eiko was sure she could handle a few girls around her age without a problem as long as she didn't let any of their insults get to her.

The lunch hall became silent. There weren't any spoons and forks clashing with each other. The remains of the mystery boxes were thrown in the trash. "I think that's our cue." Dexter stood up from the chair.

"Are you sure?" Eiko quietly spoke, sheepishly glancing behind her. When she saw that there wasn't anyone except for the glaring lunch lady there, she gave out a sigh of relief. "Alright, let's go."

The weather outside was even colder than the previous day. The gamer hadn't brought any warm clothes since she knew she could head back home during the winter vacation but she certainly hadn't expected such dramatic temperature changes. The gust of wind made her shiver but she played it off when Dexter glanced at her from the corner of his eyes.

"You remember the plan, right?" The boy seriously spoke as they walked out of the hall. "10pm, black clothes, sneakiness – stuff like that."

Eiko rolled her eyes. "Don't worry. I'm great at stealth games, trust me. I've got the best clothes ready."

"It's hard not to worry. You do know what's going to happen if we get found out, right?" He mumbled out.

"Nope. Stop talking about that. We won't get found out," she firmly said, "everything will go according to plan."

Dexter raised a brow. "If you say so…"

Chapter 6

Time passed surprisingly quickly. Eiko was far too busy delving into her imagination, making up different scenarios of her and Dexter. She hoped that things would go smoothly but… She wasn't the luckiest type. When it came down to randomness in games, she always got the short end of the straw. Then again, this was real life – she didn't actually know whether she was lucky or not. That didn't soothe her evident anxiety combined with excitement, though, and when the clock hit 10pm she jumped.

Eiko tied her hair and put on her hood and glasses, successfully concealing her head and part of her eyes. She made sure to pull the skirt down in order to hide as much as she could from her legs. The girl took a deep breath as she finally opened the door, cringing when it loudly creaked due to its old age. The sound echoed throughout the empty hallway but there weren't any students out and about. Considering the painful punishment she got due to her being a few seconds late for class, she shivered when she imagined what would happen if she got found outside. Each step was cautious and soundless as Eiko made her way to the bottom of the building. The front door was closed but it wasn't as creaky as the one leading to her room – something she was pleasantly surprised by.

The campus looked much scarier during the night. Its tall ancient walls engulfed the whole area, making it seem as if there was no escape. The two dorm buildings were threateningly high up in the air. Dead leaves crunched between careful steps and the crickets in the forest signified the only sign of life. There was only one orange light in front of the main gate; everything else had been cloaked in darkness. *If only I could use the flashlight of my phone,* Eiko sighed, making her way towards the front doors leading to the main building. Her stomach flipped in anxiety when she saw a shadow in the distance. Thankfully, as she got closer she saw that it was Dexter.

"What are you wearing?"

She didn't expect that to be the first thing that came out of the boy's mouth. "What do you mean?" Eiko folded her arms across her chest. "I'm being stealthy, duh. What are *you* wearing? You look like a hipster."

Neither of them were dressed for the occasion although Eiko knew she looked way better. She wasn't the one wearing a black beanie, matching shirt and pants. Then again… His camouflage was a bit more suitable.

"Oh please." Dexter rolled his eyes. "At least I don't look like someone who has come out of a slice of life manga."

The girl couldn't control the slight blush of embarrassment that spread across her features. "Wh—Whatever," she mumbled out, stepping over the stairs leading to the door so that her back could face Dexter. "Let's just get this over with."

"Okay," he sighed, "let's do this."

Dexter took a step closer to Eiko and waited for her to grab onto the door handle. The girl glanced at him the moment her fingers grazed it and he gave her a firm nod. After taking a deep breath, Eiko pushed the door open. There was a quiet creak that sounded but the duo continued heading inside nonetheless. The change of temperature was uncomfortable – it was colder inside than it was outside – but that was the last thing the girl wanted to complain about. The white walls were now completely black and the chilly air only made the whole situation much worse. There was no light coming from the windows.

"Be careful where you step." Dexter firmly noted as he took the lead.

Eiko followed suit, though she tried not to glance around too much. She was afraid of seeing a shape on the wall or a monster that was about to jump out of nowhere – curse her for playing all those horror games! "Are you sure you know where you're going?" She quietly asked.

Dexter looked back at her for a moment. "Don't worry," he said, "we just need to turn right and go through the first door. Here." He quickened his pace until they reached the location and without wasting any time, he grabbed the handle and pushed the door open.

The boy was the first one who took a step inside. Eiko stood on her toes so that she could see from behind his shoulder. She raised a brow in disbelief. "This... This isn't the caretaker's room."

"No, it's not." Dexter's eyes were wide in surprise. He kept looking up and down, carefully inspecting each corner of the room as if he could actually see anything in the darkness. "But it's supposed to be." He was quick to defend himself as he turned around and took a few steps backwards so that he could look at what was written on the door.

"This is Chemistry!" Eiko exclaimed, raising her voice much higher than what she intended. She instantly covered her mouth. "This is Chemistry!" She repeated, although this time it was a mere whisper.

Dexter hummed. "Maybe it's the room next to it?"

"Are we seriously going to guess where it is?" She groaned.

The boy cautiously closed the door behind him and backed away before facing Eiko. "Do you have a better idea?"

Eiko's shoulders slouched in defeat. "No, but I don't want us to get found out. It's easy for you to be so reckless when you haven't been punished yet."

"Pfft, we won't." Dexter grinned. "Where's your adventurous spirit, Eiko? I thought you were a gamer."

The girl opened her mouth to speak although no words came out. The frustration that flowed through her made her grimace and as much as she wanted to ignore the blatant teasing, she became a victim to her own emotions. "Fine," she sighed, "I'll go left. You go right. Whoever finds the room first wins."

"You're on." Dexter nodded, cracking his neck. "Let's go."

After splitting up, Eiko found herself becoming even more anxious. She tried to cool down the feeling and kept her back straight as she walked, bright eyes cautiously looking at each door. The first one she got to was Math class. She took a step closer and faced it, internally flinching upon remembering what had happen mere hours ago. The bruised skin over the top of her palms burned as if to remind her even further and Eiko had to take a deep breath. She gave herself a nod before reaching for the door handle. Thankfully, the room wasn't locked and the girl managed to take a look inside. She didn't know why she even bothered considering she had seen that it wasn't the caretaker's room, but she found herself frozen in her steps. The room itself looked peaceful, almost, when it was so empty and there was no signs of life inside. Eiko's rapid heartbeat unfroze the blood in her veins and she found herself capable of moving once more. Trying not to think too much about it, she closed the door and leaned her back against it. *What if the nun showed up?* Eiko anxiously thought. *What if I get caught and punished again? Would I be expelled? Would I be physically hurt or would I be finally free*? The girl shook her head. She knew she wasn't helping herself in any way by thinking of possible scenarios – she had to continue her task. Unlike games, there were no checkpoints she could access. Whatever she chose to do would stay with her forever. That was the scariest part of it all.

Eiko ran her hand through her hair in order to calm herself down, not realizing that she had pushed her hood away from her head. Now, her face and hair were fully exposed but she was far too nervous to notice. She started walking towards the next room that turned out to be Chemistry. After that was the Nurse's Office. She felt as if she was stuck in an endless limbo with her target becoming further and further away. The only sound that could be heard was the light tapping of her shoes, echoing throughout the empty building. Nonetheless, Eiko kept on moving as she went through each and every room in a search that became more and more hopeless after each second that passed. She wondered whether Dexter had found it already and was waiting for her to go back. *What if he has been caught?*

Before the girl could spiral into thoughts of negativity, she heard faint walking in the distance. There was no way the tapping was coming from her since she wasn't walking at that very moment. Her breath hitched in her throat and she found herself frozen in fear again. There were shivers that ran across the back of her neck, leading up to the bottom of her spine as she stared in horror at the black figure getting closer. She reached for the handle of the door on her right and cursed underneath her breath when she found out it was locked – the Nurse's Office was one of the only rooms that was locked. *So much for finding out whether I'm lucky or not*, Eiko sighed. She knew she couldn't run – she couldn't do anything. The girl felt like a deer stuck in the headlights of an incoming car; she was trapped with no escape. The only thing she could pray for was the mercy of whoever found her.

As the figure got closer, she saw that it was one of the nuns who was holding some sort of basket. It wasn't the math teacher, thankfully, thought Eiko couldn't make out her face until she got much closer. Her whole body stiffened as she waited for the figure to get closer, taking a small defensive step backwards in the process. Each second felt like a whole eternity.

"Eiko?" A familiar voice rang out. "What are you doing here? Y—You shouldn't be here!"

It was Sister Ann.

Out of all the sadistic and evil nuns, Eiko got the only one who had treated her with kindness. A quiet sigh of relief escaped her lips, though she still knew she was in trouble. "I know but... There's something I need to do. Please, *please* don't tell anyone you saw me."

As the nun got closer, Eiko saw that she was carrying multiple books inside the basket. Her brows were furrowed in worry and her lips were pursed in a small frown. "What's going on?" Sister

Ann softly asked.

The gamer found herself at a crossroad. There were two options she could take – she could either tell Sister Ann what was going on and hope that she would help her and wouldn't betray her further down the line, or she could abandon the quest and head back to her dorm in order to avoid any punishment. Eiko bit her bottom lip in frustration. *I've come so far*, she thought, *I can't give up now*!

"Are you feeling alright?" The nun took a step closer.

Her voice was enough to snap Eiko out of her thoughts. She lightly jumped and glanced up at the woman, a sheepish smile spreading across her features. "Yeah, yeah, I'm fine. It's just that… Well…" She glanced away, grabbing her wrist with her opposite hand. "I know that technology isn't allowed but… I got my phone taken by one of the students and he won't give it back no matter what I do." She looked up at Sister Ann with pleading eyes. "It's the only source of fun I have. I *need* to get it back."

"Oh…" The nun's voice trailed off. She looked confused, as if she was internally struggling with what to do. "I don't know—" She sighed. "I could try to talk to the student. What is his name?"

Eiko shook her head. "He won't give it back no matter what. He might even give it to one of the nuns if I pester him too much."

"Then what were you planning to do here so late at night?" Sister Ann quietly asked. "If you get found out you'll get in serious trouble. Please, be careful Eiko. St Ambrose isn't like the other schools... It's different in a *bad* way."

It's now or never, Eiko thought, *I need to tell her the truth, it's the only way.*

"Well..." She started, glancing away once more. Her eyes kept trailing around and she knew she looked like a kid that had been caught doing something they shouldn't have been doing in the first place. "We were planning on borrowing a key to the boy's room and getting my phone while he wasn't there," Eiko weakly spoke, "I know it's not the right thing to do but I'm desperate."

Sister Ann looked disappointed. It was a look Eiko had been given multiple times by her mother whenever she stayed up way too late playing video games – she hated it.

"We?" The nun curiously asked.

Eiko's face went pale. She shouldn't have brought Dexter into her mindless adventure. Now, if Sister

Ann decided to take action against them, they'd both get in serious trouble. "Myself and I." The girl nervously laughed. "I sometimes refer to myself as multiple people since I… Uh… I like to think of myself as a one woman army. Yeah!" Eiko tried to be as confident as she could though she internally cringed at what she was saying. Right as she was about to back away from the nun and pretend nothing had happened, she heard Dexter's voice in the distance.

"Eiko! I found the caretaker's room!" He loudly spoke.

Sister Ann raised a brow, watching Eiko cover her face with her hands as if she was trying to vanish in plain sight. Dexter lightly jogged up to the girl. When he got close enough to see the nun, though, he froze in his tracks.

"Hi," he dumbly spoke.

Sister Ann heavily sighed. "You do know that I'm the caretaker, right?"

Both Eiko and Dexter perked up. Their eyes were wide in surprise as the nun gave them a nod. Eiko looked back at Dexter with evident confusion spread across her face. Dexter gave her a shrug in order to tell her that he didn't really know.

"No, not really." Eiko defensively raised her hands. "W—We'll just get going now…" She cautiously moved away.

"Wait." Sister Ann firmly spoke. "I'll help you."

Even if Dexter was suspicious, Eiko was excited. "Really?" She slightly raised her voice, eyes bright with newfound motivation. "You'll do it?"

The warm smile that spread across the nun's features gave off hope. "You see, I'm still new here and I don't really approve of the 'No Fun Allowed' policy. I think that students should be given the chance to enjoy themselves as long as they're properly doing their school work. Now… I definitely am against 'borrowing' things that don't belong to you but I can make an exception this one time."

"How can we trust you?" Dexter asked.

Eiko nudged him in the rib with her elbow. "Oh, shut up. Don't ruin this for us!"

"What if she rats us out to the principal?" He turned to her, trying to keep his voice low.

"She won't. She's nice." The girl was quick to defend the nun.

Dexter rolled his eyes. "Everyone here is evil, Eiko.

Evil!"

"I suggest we don't waste any more time." Sister Ann joined the conversation with a light giggle. "After all, curfew was almost two hours ago. The quicker you get back to your dorms, the safer you'll be. Please follow me." The caretaker started walking in the same direction Dexter had come from. It did turn out to be true that her office was there. It was a small and narrow room with a lone cupboard, a wooden chair and a box full of keys. It looked awful compared to the other rooms. Eiko couldn't help but feel sorry for Sister Ann.

"We're looking for Christian's key," Dexter mumbled out.

The nun sat on the tiny chair and opened the box. It took her almost a full minute in order to find the needed spare key. "Christian, Christian…" She murmured beneath her breath as she carefully inspected each key. "Oh! There it is." She grabbed it and turned to the duo once again. Her lips were pursed in a victorious smile as she extended her arm, exposing the palm where the key was situated.

Eiko smiled and took a step closer so that she could gently grab it. "Thank you so much, Sister Ann. You're our savior."

"Nice." Dexter clicked his tongue.

The caretaker breathlessly giggled. "Don't worry about it. Just make sure to bring it back tomorrow before dinner time, otherwise the three of us will get in trouble."

Eiko's smiled disappeared. Dinner time was when they were going to head into Christian's room due to being sure he wouldn't be there. They couldn't skip class since they didn't want to be severely punished... "You can count on us." The girl shakily spoke, giving out a nod. "We'll head back to our dorms now. Thank you again." She bowed her head.

The duo bid their farewell and swiftly made their way out of the main school building. The weather was just as cold as it was before and all the dead leaves were still on the ground, waiting to be stepped on. The two dorm buildings looked as threatening as ever as they got closer to them. It was as if time had stopped while they were inside. The only difference was that the moon could be seen, Eiko realized when she glanced up. The light coming from it was bright and strong enough to cast a shadow. It look beautiful and otherworldly.

"I can't believe we just did that." Dexter laughed.

Eiko turned to him with a shaky smile. "I know," she breathed out, "I thought we were going to fail."

"It's time for us to get some well-deserved rest."

The boy took a deep breath and slowly let it out.

Even if she was smiling, she shook her head. "We still don't know when the best time to sneak into Christian's room is," she stated.

"Dinner time, duh," Dexter ly replied.

"No," Eiko mumbled out, "don't you remember what Sister Ann told us? We have to get the key back to the caretaker's room *before* diner time, not after."

The boy's expression was unreadable for a second. Less than a moment later, though, he slightly raised his hands to the side. "It's not going to be the only rule we've broken this week. It'll be fine, trust me."

"Trust you?" Eiko's lips twisted into a grimace. "You told me there was no way we'd get caught and look what happened! We just got lucky it was Sister Ann instead of anyone else."

"We got the key, didn't we?" Dexter was quick to defend himself. "And tomorrow you'll have your phone back. I don't know why you're complaining."

The girl rolled her eyes. "I'm not complaining, I'm saying that you shouldn't be so confident when you don't know what will happen."

"But I do know," Dexter sighed, "you'll be thanking me tomorrow."

Eiko folded her arms across her chest, raising a brow in suspicion. "Sure, sure. We'll see." She started walking towards the dorms. "Let's get going."

Everything felt like an illusion – it was as if Eiko had taken control of her dreams for once. She couldn't believe she actually broke into St Ambrose and managed to convince a staff member to lend her an item that didn't belong to her in the first place. The girl's hand was shaky as she unlocked the door and stepped inside. When she removed her shoes and ran over to her bed in order to plop onto it, grab her pillow and scream out of happiness, she still couldn't believe it was all *real*. Despite the fact that the school seemed like it had come out of a circle from hell – all the teachers were evil, all the students were trapped inside – Eiko felt happy for once. Her hands no longer burned from the punishment she had received earlier in the day. She was no longer anxious and a slave to her own negative thoughts; she felt light and free. It was as if she had been reborn.

Chapter 7

Eiko was never a troublemaker in school. She didn't really fit the stereotype. Instead, she was the quiet girl always playing on her phone in the corner. Most students didn't care about her which was both a good and bad thing. After all, she never got bullied but never got any good friends during her last year. The teachers felt the same way most of the time, so long as they didn't catch her playing on the device during class. Now? Things were different. She had met Dexter and together they had formed a powerful team. Eiko believed that if they were inside a video game, they'd be unstoppable. Life kept becoming more and more like a set of rules, programed to lead her to her fate – whatever *that* was. Right now, though, she needed to get back her phone. Had she been alone, she never would've followed such a reckless and dangerous plan but in the end she was glad she did.

Even if she was even close to falling asleep, Eiko knew she had to do her best. The adrenaline ran strong through her veins and her mind was attacked by exciting thoughts about tomorrow. Dealing with Christian wouldn't be that bad, right? He wasn't a staff member and couldn't do anything other than hit Dexter and her if he managed to find out. It would be impossible for him to tell any of the teachers after the phone was back in Eiko's hands as well, since he would get punished for keeping secrets *and* having technology in his possession. The girl smirked as she glanced up at the ceiling, amused at the imaginary scenario. She covered herself with the futon, not bothering to remove her current clothes. *I shouldn't get that ahead of myself,* she thought, *things have gone well so far but there's still a chance everything might go wrong.* Eiko shook her head. *Damn it! I'll be positive for once. There's nothing wrong with that.*

Before she knew it, she had drifted off to sleep. It wasn't until the familiar yet painful alarm noise coming from the clock on the desk did EIko finally wake up from her deep slumber. She opened her eyes and grimaced at the device, trying to cover her ears with the pillow. When she realized it wouldn't be enough to block the obnoxious ringing, though, she got up and manually turned it off. It didn't take her long to remember what was supposed to happen. The excitement made the evident sleepiness fade away and Eiko was almost ten full minutes earlier to class – this wasn't something that often happened, even when she was on the verge of being painfully punished, although there she was, sitting on the desk in the far back with a wide grin spread across her features. She couldn't pay attention in class no matter how hard she tried, though she still did her best to write everything down. Much to her annoyance, time passed by extremely slow. Even if she prayed and prayed, it seemed as if time itself had stopped. Each time she looked at the round clock on the upper part of the wall over the blackboard, thinking that hours have passed, she saw that instead of hours it was mere minutes. Each time Eiko got extremely disappointed. She didn't even search for Dexter like she had before – she wanted dinner time to come already so that they could get it over with.

All bad things would come to an end no matter how long and painful they might be. After the school bell rang, the gamer almost jumped out of her seat, grabbed her backpack and made her way to the front gate. She leaned against the school wall, eyes locked onto the entrance as they carefully studied each student that passed. Kate and her groupies were the first one to exit the school. After them, the jocks showed up, led by Christian himself. Eiko had to hide her face in order to not make herself be seen. The last thing she wanted was for a fight between him and Kate again. The jocks passed by without taking note of the girl on the side. The rest of the students weren't anything special; they blended in with each other, slowly walking with slouched shoulders and frowns. They looked extremely miserable. Before Eiko had time to feel sorry for them, though, she saw Dexter's face in the distance.

Her lips curled into a wide smile and her eyes widened in excitement. She frantically waved at him in order to make her position be known. Dexter was surprised at first even as he quickened his pace in order to reach her faster.

"It's time!" Eiko squeaked.

Dexter chuckled. "Calm down, don't act so happy." He glanced behind his back for a moment. "We don't want people to be suspicious."

Despite giving a sigh of frustration in reply, Eiko knew he had a point. She took a deep breath and felt her emotions go to her stomach. "Okay," she mumbled out, "it's time."

"Do you have the key?" Dexter looked back at her.

The girl nodded, rummaging through the pockets of her coat. The key quietly jiggled as she held it up with her index finger. "Everything's here."

"Alright." Dexter rolled his shoulders and cracked his neck. He lightly pushed up his glasses when they fell beneath his nose. "I'll stay on the bench in front of the boys' dorms until Christian gets out."

Eiko raised a brow in confusion. "Okay but… What about me?"

"It'll be weird if we're seen together again," he

started, "we don't want Christian to find out about our plan. You should head to the girls' dorms and wait for me to give you the sign."

"What sign?" The gamer grumbled with a frown. "We haven't talked about any signs or stuff like that."

Dexter glanced away. "Uh huh… I'll just head over to you."

Eiko's frown instantly disappeared. As much as she didn't want to make fun of him, she still breathlessly giggled. "Nice 'sign', Dexter," she smugly commented, "you're a true leader."

The boy's face became flushed in embarrassment. He turned around so that he could hide his features. "Yeah, yeah. J—Just wait for me, alright?"

"Whatever you say," Eiko ly stated.

She cautiously started making her way back to the girls' dorms. When she spotted Kate's group chatting in front of the door leading to the interior, though, she slowed her pace even further and kept glancing around, acting like she hadn't seen them. Even if she wanted to run away the same way she had been last time Kate got ahold of her, she'd just bring unwanted attention to herself which could possibly lead to the failure of the mission. A quiet sigh of anxiety escaped thin lips as Eiko made her way closer, bracing for whatever was about to happen.

"Oh, it's Eiko," Kate loudly spoke, instantly turning around. The girl that was talking to her stopped and glanced over to the gamer. All eyes were set on Eiko and she felt their gaze burn daggers into her whole body. She folded her arms across her chest in order to protect herself and did her best to give the group a polite smile.

"H—Hey," Eiko mumbled out.

Kate's lips curled into a wide grin. "What're you doing here? It's dinner time, isn't it?"

The gamer mentally rolled her eyes. *I could ask you the same thing*, she thought. Instead of being smug about it, though, Eiko kept her sheepish persona. "I was just about to head back in order to change my undershirt. I wouldn't miss dinner for the world. Could you... maybe let me through?"

"Maybe you should start skipping dinner if you can't get through us." Kate laughed.

Eiko felt her cheeks redden and her stomach turn from the awful comment. If she felt self-conscious about her looks before, now she fully hated herself. "Maybe..." she shakily spoke, trying to keep her eyes from watering. Tears of frustration were hard to fight against – Eiko was an angry crier. Each time she lost, she felt like crying.

The other girls joined Kate in laughing at Eiko who tightly shut her eyes and gritted her teeth, praying that Dexter would show up soon. *Wait,* she suddenly thought, *if they see us together then they'll start spreading rumors. Ugh, school sucks. There's no way I can win here no matter how hard I try.*

"Ew, it's Christian." Kate suddenly stopped. She was no longer smiling – instead, she was now carrying a grimace of disgust. "Let me just grab my handbag," she said, "then we'll head over to the lunch hall. I don't want him to take my spot like last time."

Eiko felt completely out of place. She didn't know whether the bully was done with her or not; it was as if she suddenly didn't exist. She almost didn't hear Kate talk about Christian due to her trying to battle her negative thoughts and tears. When Kate and her groupies walked away, though, Eiko let out a breath she hadn't realized she had been holding and turned around in order to make her way back to the boys' dorms. There she saw Dexter waving at her with a smile spread across his features. Considering how happy he looked, he certainly had managed to escape the bully's wrath, unlike her.

You win some, you lose some…

"Are you ready?" Dexter walked up to her. The moment he saw how shaky she was being, his smile disappeared and his brows got furrowed in worry. "Hey," he quickly spoke, "is everything alright?"

Eiko wiped her eyes with the sleeve of her coat to make sure that none of her tears would escape before giving him a firm nod. "Y—Yeah, it's fine. I'm fine. Let's go," she weakly mumbled out.

"If you say so…" The boy quietly said, motioning for her to follow. They walked up the stairs in silence; the only sound that could be heard was from their heavy steps. Eiko's eyes were locked onto the ground and she kept trailing behind. She was far too busy thinking about Kate's words – even if she wanted to forget them, even if she knew that she was letting her win by getting hurt, she couldn't control her emotions. She didn't even want her phone back at that very moment, she just wanted to go home to her parents and spend the next year just playing video games. Unfortunately, reality was far from being kind.

"Oof, sorry," Eiko murmured when she accidentally bumped into Dexter.

He hummed, giving a shrug of his shoulders. "We're here," he finally spoke, trying to keep his voice down. "It's now or never."

The girl sighed. "Yeah," she mumbled out before taking out the small key. Despite its irrelevant size, its weight was heavy in her hand. She took a deep breath and slowly unlocked the door. It creaked open; the sound was loud and echoed throughout the whole building. Eiko felt a shiver run down her spine as she stepped inside. She didn't know what to expect – her mind had been torturing her the whole day. She was surprised to see that his room was almost the same as hers, except for a few posters of bands across the wall near his bed. Everything else blended with the walls. Even if she was sure Christian wouldn't come back, she couldn't stop herself from imagining all awful scenarios of him finding out and her and Dexter getting expelled.

"Where do you think he put it?" Dexter asked. His voice successfully took Eiko out of her thoughts.

She glanced around, taking in each detail of the small confined room. "I don't know," she said as she took a step closer to the bed. "Maybe here?" She knelt in front of the bed stand and pulled open the first drawer. It was completely empty. "Nope," she sighed.

"It might be on the desk." Dexter walked over to said location and leaned over it, looking for any sort of clue. His shoulders slouched in defeat when he couldn't find anything. "Do you think he's always been carrying it?"

Eiko shook her head. "There's no way. He wouldn't risk getting found out and punished."

"Yeah, I guess you're right," Dexter hummed.

"Did you check the cupboard?" Eiko walked away from the bed and made her way towards Dexter. "Here." She leaned forwards and reached for the small cupboard underneath the desk. It clicked open and upon seeing what was inside, she gave out a sigh of relief. "It's here. Oh my god, I can't believe it!"

The boy gasped in surprise. "Really? Ha, I told you!" He smiled. "There was no reason for you to worry so much."

"I guess…" Eiko's voice trailed off. She swiftly grabbed the phone and held it close to her chest as she closed the cupboard with free hand. "We should go. Don't want to risk Christian finding us out at the end."

Dexter clicked his tongue. "Yup, you've got a point. Dinner time will be over soon, we need to head back and grab something to eat too."

After making sure everything looked the same way

it had before their arrival, Eiko opened the front door. Halfway through her exit, though, she heard a quiet whisper come out of Dexter behind her. She quickly turned around, eyes wide in confusion. "Huh? What'd you say?"

"Look at this." The boy knelt down in front of the trashcan next to the door. He picked up the ripped piece of paper and stood up again, holding it close to his face so that he could properly read it.

"What is it?" Eiko asked, taking a step closer and stood on her toes so that she could see what was written on it.

Dexter's voice was low as he spoke, "St Ambrose's Principal is accused of…"

"Of what?" The girl was quick to ask. "Come on, now's not the time to keep me on edge. I already feel nervous as it is!"

"I don't know what it is. It's ripped apart – I can't read the rest of it. Do you think it's in the bin?" He glanced behind her.

Eiko gave a shrug. "It's empty, I already checked while I was looking for my phone."

"Why would Christian have a piece of a newspaper in the first place?" Dexter mumbled out. "We should take it for safekeeping."

"Are you crazy?" The gamer frowned. "We shouldn't touch anything in the room. Let's just *go*." She grabbed him by the wrist and pulled him along. Unfortunately for her, though, she didn't know whether Dexter had taken the paper. Eiko just wanted to get back to her room, charge her phone and play games throughout the whole night. She was missing on so many quests, she had to catch up ASAP!

The girl tightly held onto Dexter throughout their journey to the bottom floor. When they got outside, she put her phone in the pocket of her coat and fixed her glasses, trying to make herself look as presentable as possible even if the cold sweat across her forehead made her bangs stick to her face. She knew they needed to act as casual and as normal as they could but she couldn't help the smile that had spread across her features.

"We can say that this mission was a success," Dexter proudly spoke.

Eiko giggled. "Definitely. Now I just need to hide my phone from, well, pretty much everyone. I don't want the same thing to happen again," she sighed, "you go on ahead. I'll stop by the caretaker's room to return the key."

"Are you sure you won't get lost again?" The boy raised a brow.

Eiko rolled her eyes and gave him a wave of goodbye. Even if she was extremely happy, she still got annoyed whenever Dexter wanted to be smug. The walk to Sister Ann's room was much quicker now that she actually knew where it was located. The girl tried to ignore the way her tummy kept rumbling, showing her that it needed food. Most of the school halls were now empty, except for different staff members. Each time Eiko passed by a nun or a priest, she instantly glanced away, grit her teeth and prayed that they wouldn't stop and ask questions. It didn't seem that they cared, though. Upon getting to the caretaker's room, the girl tried to get it over with as quick as possible. Unfortunately for her, the door was locked. A sigh of defeat escaped her lips and she leaned back against the wall, eyes curiously glancing around, looking for Sister Ann. As the minutes passed, Eiko kept checking her phone in order to look at the time. Dinner was going to be over soon and she felt hungrier than ever but she knew she couldn't move away until she gave the key back. After all, Sister Ann had trusted her. The least she could do was hold her end of the deal.

By the time the nun showed up, Eiko's phone had completely died and the sun had fully set, leaving the school building in almost complete darkness. The gamer perked up when she heard steps coming towards her. She glanced at the figure from the ground – she had sat in front of the door and held her knees close to her chest, almost falling asleep while waiting. The girl's knees quietly popped as she stood up with a smile, looking expectantly at Sister Ann. "I've got the key," she murmured, extending one arm holding the item.

Sister Ann looked… reluctant; surprised, even. "What are you doing here?" She quietly spoke, frantically looking around as if searching for an invisible foe. "Y—You shouldn't be here," she whispered, brows furrowed in worry and lips frowning.

Eiko couldn't help but raise a brow – she had no idea what was going on. She hadn't expected the nun to act so paranoid. "Don't you remember?" The gamer tilted her head to the side in confusion. "You gave me the key last night when I uh… 'Met' you."

"What key might you be talking about?"

There was suddenly an unknown male voice. It was deep and raspy as if it belonged to someone who had smoked throughout their entire life. It was scary, to say the least. Eiko couldn't control the way she instantly stiffened in fear and hid the key she was holding without even thinking about it. A man formed out of the shadows, looming over Sister Ann as if he was a ghost manifesting out of thin air

– it didn't help that the hallway was dark. He was extremely tall and thin with sunken cheeks and wrinkles all around his face. He was wearing the standard uniform of a priest, although his hair was lacking and the white thick moustache over the top of his lip made him seem even more ancient. He looked like death incarnate – Eiko hadn't even seen him before and she was glad for it. Then again, judging by his scary demeanor and firm voice, she knew that both her and Sister Ann were in trouble. *If only I was faster and actually listened to her,* Eiko sadly thought, glancing to the ground in shame. She knew that whatever was going to happen wasn't going to be anything good. If the worst came to fruit, though, she would defend the young nun with everything she had, including taking blame for the events that had transpired. She didn't want someone innocent to get hurt, despite her being an accomplice. Sister Ann was completely frozen. Her eyes were empty and void of life as she mindlessly stared at Eiko, lips slightly quivering as if she was mentally battling herself on what to say. The priest stood there, unmoving, waiting for any of the females to explain themselves.

"… I lost the key to my room," the gamer quietly started, trying to keep her voice from shaking, "and Sister Ann was kind enough to help me find it."

The priest didn't look convinced at all. A quiet hum

escaped his lips and after the awkward yet tense silence had taken its hold over the trio once more, Eiko realized that he was waiting on her to continue.

"It was my fault," she said, "I should have been more careful. I—I know that there aren't any spare keys for the students and—and I promise I'll be more careful next time."

"What do you have to say about this, Sister Ann?" He slowly asked, placing his hand over the nun's shoulder.

She instantly flinched from the touch. "Eiko is a good student. She is well-mannered and polite. I felt it was my duty to help the bright future of St Ambrose," she robotically spoke, "sometimes we all need a little push. It was all in the Lord's name."

Another hum could be heard in reply, though the man's expression was difficult to read – he had no expression at all. The poker face he carried made him look even more horrifying. Eiko couldn't look at him for longer than a few seconds each time. "Very well then," he finally spoke and removed his hand. Sister Ann's shoulders instantly slouched. "If this happens again, you will both be punishment."

The last thing that came out of his mouth was the threatening statement as he turned around and walked away, disappearing into the same shadows he came from. When he was gone, the gamer still felt as if she was being watched. She realized that Sister Ann's paranoid behavior didn't come out of the blue – she had a good reason to be afraid. Without wanting to spend any more time in the cursed main building, Eiko quickly handed the key over to the nun and half-jogged all the way to the entrance. When she got outside, she was heavily panting as if she had run a marathon. The anxiety and fear were still present in her body but at least she didn't feel hungry anymore. Her phone's presence was soothing in her pocket, although before the happiness could set its way inside her, the awful thought of the priest finding out about it manifested first. She felt a shiver run down her spine and wrapped her arms around herself, trying to keep the heat from disappearing out of her body. Needless to say, Eiko was completely exhausted. She barely managed to walk up the stairs to the last floor in order to get to her room; her knees hurt, her thighs were burning and it was difficult to breathe. She had to stop a few seconds in order to catch her breath and wipe the sweat from her forehead. When she heard Kate's voice echo throughout the staircase, though, she used her newfound motivation born from her flight or fight response and finally reached her room. The first thing she did upon getting inside was to plop onto her bed. Even if the mattress was hard and uncomfortable, she felt like it was the best thing ever. Her exhausted body begged for her to call it a night and sleep, though Eiko had to start charging her phone before doing anything else. Now that she had her favorite device back she felt at ease but her thoughts kept trailing off to the priest that had almost caught her. *Who was that person?* The girl shook her head, deciding that it would be in vain trying to figure out who he was – all her classes so far had been led by nuns, not priests. Eiko slowly stood up from the bed and made her way towards the desk. Her body felt heavy which is why she had to sit on the chair in order to reach for her suitcase and pull out the phone's charger. She carefully untangled it and, after making sure the device's screen showed that it was charging, she placed it on the corner of the desk and held her head in her hands. *I can't believe this*, she thought, *it's only my second day at St Ambrose and yet… So many things have already happened. It's overwhelming. Maybe I could finally get Dexter to play with me. I still haven't been to the school's library so I don't know how much space there is but it should be fine. Then again… they'll most likely take my game away.* Eiko put her forehead against the desk and gave out a loud sigh of frustration, hands ruffling the sides of her hair. She didn't care that her hairstyle would get ruined; she was heading to bed soon anyway. The girl was taken out of her thoughts by the loud rumbling of her stomach. She pushed herself into a proper sitting position once more and glanced down at her stomach in sadness.

"Not now," she quietly mumbled out, "we'll eat tomorrow. I promise."

It didn't seem that her body liked the idea, though, if the loud piercing pain in her tummy was anything to go by. The gamer cautiously stood up from the desk, holding most of her weight on her hands before moving away. She didn't know whether her body was tired from the lack of sleep due to her excitement for the mission, the big amount of stairs she had to climb a few times each day or from the fading adrenaline. It didn't matter to her – she just wanted to sleep and ignore the pain. The girl did her best to change in her sleeping gown as fast as she could so that she could finally head to bed. Unlike last night where she was kept awake by countless thoughts running through her head, she fell asleep the moment her head hit the pillow.

Despite easily falling asleep, Eiko was plagued by nightmares throughout the whole night. All those different yet frightening scenarios suddenly started manifesting in her dreams. In the beginning she thought Christian had caught her and Dexter and had called the principal. That was the first time she woke up in cold sweat. The second time her mind replayed the meeting she had with the bad priest, except that this time Sister Ann got in trouble and lost her job because of her. The whole school ended up knowing and despising Eiko for what she had done.

The nightmares kept replaying themselves over and over again, and the girl found it impossible to stay asleep for more than two hours each time – if the clock quietly clicking over the desk was anything to go by. The fear and frustration combined made her heartbeat quicken and prevent her from easily falling back asleep. A part of her didn't want to; she didn't want to have any more nightmares even if her sleep-deprived body begged her to let it rest for once. The whole night was an awful experience. Eiko hadn't realized how much the past events had scarred her and she couldn't help but think that there was something extremely off about St Ambrose. Yes, the staff were sadistic and cruel. Most of the students were either bullies or extremely nihilistic but there had to be something else…. She couldn't quite put her finger on it.

Chapter 8

It was nice not to be woken up by the annoying loud sounds of the alarm. When Eiko opened her eyes, she saw that the sun was brightly shining in her room, a bright line going sideways through the room. There was confusion at first. *Why is the sun so high up so early?* Eiko grumpily thought, *I can't believe it's actually bright outside.* She grimaced upon glancing at the source of light and covered her eyes with her hand as she pushed herself into a sitting position. A quiet yawn escaped her lips, tired eyes cautiously glancing over to the alarm clock. It was completely still and quiet – a welcome change in the girl's hectic life. As she finally got out of the bed and made her way to the desk, she grabbed her phone, unlocked it and instantly checked the calendar. Her eyes widened in surprise. The screen showed 'Saturday'.

"Wow..." Eiko quietly spoke, "I can't believe I survived my first week of school."

The gamer couldn't help but smile. Even if St Ambrose was a very sadistic school, she still felt some sort of accomplishment. Eiko knew she was still very far from getting used to the way things worked and considering the fact that she seemed to attract trouble wherever she went, she believed she would be punished over and over again but... She was still happy.

"Now I just need to survive the rest of the year," she sighed, finally putting her phone down. As much as she wanted to stay in her room all day and catch up on her games, she knew she had to get breakfast first. Skipping dinner had turned out to be a mistake; she felt lightheaded and slightly sick. Each time she stood up her vision blacked for a few seconds and she almost lost her balance. The air in the room was warm for once, the girl couldn't help but notice as she made her way to the bathroom. Her morning rituals that consisted of brushing her teeth and washing her face with ice cold water in order to fully wake herself up finished soon enough, and after she changed into her uniform and put her hair up with her favorite pink bow, she made her way downstairs. Despite not knowing whether the clothes were required during the weekend where there was no school, Eiko still didn't want to risk getting yelled at.

Upon getting outside, the gamer saw that most students were already up. All benches around the campus were occupied by group of friends that blended into the dull buildings behind them. At least Eiko turned out to be right about the uniform – it was always mandatory. She should have expected as much from St Ambrose and its endless set of both written and unwritten rules. Thankfully, there was no sign of Kate or Christian anywhere nearby, which is why Eiko was able to freely make her way to the lunch hall. The vast room itself wasn't as full as it usually was during diner time, though there was still a good amount of people present. There was a faint smell of vanilla sugar lingering in the air that made the girl salivate. Even if she knew that sweets weren't the best way to start the day, she couldn't tear her eyes off from the set of big muffins hidden beneath the glass. The girl got closer without even realizing it as if she was hypnotized by the delicious smell. There were three lines of muffins, all of which had a different color. The furthest left were the vanilla-flavored sweets, then there were the chocolate and last, but not least, were the strawberry. Eiko wanted to try them all but after missing dinner last night, she knew that stuffing herself with carbohydrates wasn't the best idea. *Just one wouldn't hurt…*

Despite it being the weekend, the lunch lady wasn't impressed. The gamer knew she couldn't blame her, though, because if she had to work seven days a week she would be grumpy as well. The woman's voice was tired and groggy as she told Eiko to hurry up with her order because there were other students waiting. When the girl glanced behind her in order to check, she didn't see anyone. It was obvious that the employee just wanted to get it done and over with. Taking a deep breath, Eiko forced herself to a fake but friendly smile.

"I'll have one vanilla muffin, please," she politely stated.

The woman groaned as if she had been asked the impossible. Nonetheless, she reached for one of the sweets with her gloved hand, not bothering to look which one she was taking. Unfortunately for Eiko, she was given a chocolate muffin. "That'll be $1.99," the lunch lady commanded.

"Uhm…" Eiko mumbled out, not sure how to continue. She stared at the muffin then back at the lunch lady, still carrying her smile. "I asked for vanilla…"

"That'll be $1.99."

The girl's shoulders slouched in defeat. It was difficult to communicate with people who didn't want to help you despite that being their job. Without saying anything else, Eiko rummaged through the pockets of her uniform until she managed to grab the cash, placed it on the counter and got her new chocolate muffin in return. The gamer absolutely loved vanilla even if chocolate was much sweeter – she wasn't a big fan of too sugary foods due to the awful sugar rush *and* sugar crash she always got. Then again… All the muffins most likely had vast amounts of sugar either way, regardless of the flavor.

Without thinking too much about it, Eiko made her way towards one of the tables in the back. Despite her being glad for not seeing Kate or Christian, the one person she actually wanted to meet wasn't there either. The best thing she could do was wait and hope that he would somehow show up even if she was certain she had slept in a lot and most students had already had breakfast. Needless to say, she was surprised when she saw Dexter enter the lunch hall, hair even messier than it usually was. He looked awful – it was as if he hadn't slept at all. There were heavy bags underneath his eyes that Eiko could see even from the vast distance between them. It didn't seem that he noticed her, though, as he made his way to the lunch lady. Even if she couldn't hear the conversation, she still saw the way he sighed in defeat when the woman got the wrong thing. Unlike her, he didn't try to fight it. Instead, he grabbed the piece of cheese pizza, turned around and started looking at the free tables.

The gamer raised one of her arms so that she could give out her position. She was holding the muffin with her free hand and took a small bite out of it. The sugar melted in her mouth and she sighed in contempt. It didn't take long for Dexter to see her. He perked up and tried to give her a smile that didn't reach his tired eyes. When he sat down in front of Eiko with a loud thud, dropping all of his weight over the chair, she couldn't help but give out a loud hum, mentally asking him to say what was wrong. It didn't look like he got the cue, though, and instead of starting a conversation or saying a simple 'Hello', he instantly dug into his pizza.

"Good morning to you too, Dexter." Eiko gritted her teeth in frustration.

The boy looked up from his pizza. "It's actually the afternoon," he coolly stated.

"Yeah, yeah." The gamer rolled her eyes before taking another bite from the sweet muffin. "What happened to you?"

Dexter sighed, "What do you mean?"

Is he seriously going to act dumb, she was getting more and more frustrated. "You look half-dead is what I'm saying." There was no reason for her to play nice if he wasn't going to answer properly.

"I feel half-dead." The boy shrugged.

"Why?" Eiko asked.

Dexter stayed silent until he finished the rest of his pizza piece. It didn't look good at all – the dough was much thicker and the toppings were non-existent. It looked as if he was eating raw bread with some cheese sprayed on top of it. Eiko couldn't imagine it actually tasting good, unlike the sugar bomb she was currently consuming.

"I couldn't sleep at all last night," he mumbled out, staring at the table.

Eiko suddenly remembered all the awful nightmares she had throughout the whole night. She shook her head, trying to get rid of the negative memories. "You and me both... Then again, I think I managed to sleep at least a little bit. I don't feel that tired but it might be from the sugar."

"I just," Dexter groaned and glanced up at the ceiling, "I dunno... I kept thinking about the piece of newspaper we saw. What was it for? What did the principal get accused for?" He lowered his voice and leaned in. "Why was it in Christian's room? There are just too many questions."

"I can't believe you're still thinking about that," Eiko murmured, eyes narrowing down in disappointment.

Dexter glanced away. "Of course I still am. There's something going on—we need to find out what it is."

"We already almost got in trouble once and

managed to leave unscathed. Do you *really* want us to get punished?" Eiko took another bite out of her muffin.

The boy completely ignored her statement. "You said that Christian was acting weird, right? What was he like?"

The girl stiffened. She flinched when she remembered the verbal fight between him and Kate. "It wasn't weird in a way of him being suspicious, though…" She defended herself. "I think he was trying to protect me from Kate?" Eiko tilted her head to the side, asking herself the question. "I don't know. I don't really want to talk about it."

"Who's Kate?" Dexter raised a brow.

Eiko nervously laughed and waved her hand around. "You don't want to know, trust me. Anyway, I don't think Christian has anything to do with what we found."

"Then what was the paper doing there?" The boy grumpily asked, folding his arms across his chest. "Why are you even defending that bully?"

"I'm not!" Eiko suddenly raised his voice. Before she continued, though, she gave out a loud sigh. "You're just looking for trouble right now."

Dexter suddenly perked up. "Oh, I know! We could

ask Sister Ann about it. She seems nice."

Eiko felt a cold shiver run down her spine upon thinking of the priest who had interrupted her and the nun's conversation. "M—Maybe we shouldn't…" She shakily spoke. "She almost got in trouble because of me."

"What happened?" The excitement in the boy's voice died down. His brows were now furrowed in worry.

The gamer stood silent for a moment, trying to think of the best way to describe the situation. There wasn't much she could say about it. "When I was returning the key I saw this… Tall, bald man. He was very creepy – and I mean *very* creepy." She took a deep breath. "He started asking Sister Ann and then me about what we were doing… Stuff like that. I had to come up with a lie on the spot but I don't think he bought it…" Her voice trailed off. "The weird thing is that he actually let us go without a punishment."

"Tall bald man, huh?" Dexter put his hand on his chin and thoughtfully hummed. "Are you talking about Father Fitzgerald?"

Eiko shrugged. "I don't know, I haven't had any classes with him yet. I hope I never have to see him again."

"You will soon. He teaches Theology and is very scary in class. I guess he's the same way out of class too," Dexter said.

"I don't want to think about it, ugh," Eiko whined, holding her head with her hands.

Before she could finish complaining about Father Fitzgerald, Dexter stood up from the table. His expression of defeat and confusion was long gone. Instead, it was replaced by a confident smirk. The gamer didn't know what that look meant but she certainly knew it wouldn't be anything good. Each time Dexter got confident, something bad always happened. Then again, she always ended up being dragged along since they were friends. Even if she did want to scold him for being so reckless, she was aware that he was the reason she had her phone back. Maybe Dexter wasn't so bad after all.

"What are you doing?" She quietly asked.

The boy ran a hand through his hair as his smirk became even wider. "*We* are going to the library."

Despite rolling her eyes out of annoyance, Eiko stood up nonetheless and followed him all the way to the inner part of the main building. She kept telling herself that she only helped him because she wanted to see what the library looked like and each time he got smug about it, she scolded him.

Thankfully, it didn't take them long to reach their destination. The library itself was just as plain as the rest of St Ambrose. The first thing Eiko saw was the wooden door with a yellow sign saying 'LIBRARY'. Upon entering, the illusion of the vast magical place was ruined. It didn't look nor feel like a school's library at all – there was a faint smell of cleaning supplies in the air as the girl cautiously walked around, eyes scanning and taking in each detail. There were two wide desks and nine chairs. The rest of the available space was occupied by tall cupboards and the librarian's desk. *There's no way I'll be able to bring a tabletop game without being found out*, Eiko sadly thought, *the librarian has a clear view*. Just as she was about to comment, she realized that Dexter was nowhere to be seen. The gamer instantly stiffened, though her shock didn't last long when she saw him making his way over to the librarian's desk.

The librarian herself looked just like she had imagined. The woman was chubby and old, had sharp-framed glasses and red lipstick. Even if she was wearing nun clothes she looked different from the others due to her face being painted. Nonetheless, she still acted the same way – she was slow when she turned around from her in order to glare at Dexter. Her voice was low and raspy as she spoke and Eiko couldn't hear anything she said.

Wait... Eiko suddenly thought. *Is that an actual computer?* Her eyes widened in surprise and she instantly perked up. *Are there more?* She instantly forgot about Dexter and their reasoning for heading in the library in the first place. The gamer was far too excited about the mere possibility of there being at least one device she could use. Much to her surprise, she saw two much smaller desks hidden behind one of the cupboards. Both of them had ancient big monitors, dusty keyboards and mice. The boxes of the computers were hidden behind the desks. Eiko couldn't help but loudly squeal in happiness. The loud sound echoed throughout the library and she had to cover her mouth after realizing her mistake. She swiftly made her way back to Dexter and the librarian. Unfortunately for her, though, they were both giving her a judgmental look. The gamer had a sheepish smile spread across her features as she excused herself and exited the room. It was better to wait for her friend outside than to continue making a fool out of herself. *It's not my fault!* Eiko leaned against the wall and folded her arms across her chest. *I didn't expect this at all... This is awesome! There's still hope for me.*

Less than five minutes later, the wooden door creaked open and Dexter walked out of the library. When Eiko glanced up at him, she saw that he was carrying multiple newspapers. Before she could ask him what they were, he beat her to it with a tired sigh.

"The librarian was so…" He stopped mid-sentence, trying to find the right word. "*Enthusiastic* about helping me, especially after you made that weird screech."

The girl glanced away from embarrassment, trying to hide her reddened cheeks. "I—I couldn't help myself, okay?!" She defensively spoke. "I never thought there'd be computers here."

"Good luck sweet-talking the librarian into letting you use them for more than five minutes," Dexter coldly stated. "Come on, let's get back to my room so that we can go through these. I need to return them tomorrow morning."

Eiko slightly stiffened. "Your room?" She mumbled out. "We could go through them in the library, right?"

"It'll take us far too long." Dexter shook his head. "Plus I think the librarian hates you."

A sigh of defeat escaped the girl's lips. "But if people see us going to your room together…" Her cheeks heated up again.

"D—Don't make it weird!" The boy suddenly raised his voice. He almost dropped the papers out of shock. "No one will even care, trust me." He glanced away, hiding his face behind the newspapers.

"Every time you say 'trust me' I feel like strangling you," Eiko lowered her voice. The embarrassment she felt was replaced by frustration. "Alright, let's get going then…"

There was an awkward silence that followed. It was uncomfortable and foreign to the often bickering duo. A part of the gamer blamed herself for making them hanging out feel weird, although she knew it was Dexter's fault for having such a bold proposition. They were teenagers, after all, and both of them got bullied every day. People would have a field day if they started assuming about their non-existent relationship. Then again… Eiko didn't have much of a choice. It was far too late to back down now. The girl's paranoia grew with every second the closer they got to the boys' dorms. Nonetheless, she kept her head down and secretly kept glancing around – it didn't seem like any of the other students cared. Most of them were sleeping in whereas the others were just trying to relax and not worry about anything considering how stressful St Ambrose was. Of course, the relief Eiko felt wouldn't last any longer. Right as they started going up the stairs, she froze in her tracks the moment she heard a familiar voice coming from upstairs. The moment Dexter was about to unlock the door leading to his room, his shoulders slouched in defeat and she hugged the vast amount of newspapers close to his chest.

Out of all the people we could've met, she grumpily thought and mentally rolled her eyes, *it just had to be Christian.*

"What're you doin' here, loser?" The bully smugly spoke. "Finally decided to start studying?"

Dexter craned his neck, glaring at Christian. He was frowning and his brows were furrowed in frustration; it was obvious he didn't want to deal with him right now, which only motivated the bully further, much to the boy's annoyance. "Not now, Christian," he weakly spoke, "I'm busy."

"Yeah," he chuckled, "you better start getting busy or you won't pass the school year. So much for me callin' you a nerd. You're just as bad as your grades."

Eiko couldn't believe what she was hearing. Dexter had bad grades? *There's no way... Christian must be lying in order to make him feel bad*, she thought. The cosplayer gave off a smartass vibe – those people usually had perfect grades, right? It just made no sense. Even so, she took a small step backwards in order to try to hide herself from

Christian's view. If he was solely focused on Dexter, then he wouldn't easily notice her. She knew she had to use that to her advantage.

"What do you want?" Despite the boy's voice being quiet and weak, there was a hint of anger hidden in his tone.

Christian shrugged as he went down the rest of the stairs. He was now fully facing Dexter – the size difference between them was vast, that much was obvious. Christian didn't look like a middle school student; he resembled a high school one, if anything. Even if Dexter was visibly intimidated and uncomfortable from the whole situation, he still stood his ground and didn't back away. "I just wanna stop seein' you're ugly mug, Dexter." The bully laughed. "Is that so much to ask?"

The cosplayer weakly sighed, "Then why don't you let me get in my room? You're the one who's prolonging having to look at my face, you know?"

There was suddenly a loud bang. Eiko couldn't help but flinch upon hearing it. When she glanced up, she saw that Christian had punched the door right next to Dexter's face. Her stomach dropped in anxiety and she felt like running away, though she knew she couldn't abandon her friend no matter what happened. They had been through so much.

Dexter had hugged the newspapers even tighter than before and it seemed as if he was trying to hide his face behind them. Christian finally managed to realize what exactly it was that the cosplayer was holding. The frustration the bully felt instantly faded away and was replaced by confusion. "These aren't study books," he dumbly stated, raising a brow. "What are you trying to do?" Christian slightly backed away after removing his hand from the door.

"I'm looking for something," the boy mumbled out.

The bully folded his arms across his chest, waiting for Dexter to continue with his statement. When he didn't, though, he gave out a heavy sigh. "And what exactly it is you're lookin' for?" Despite it being a question, he made it sound like a statement. He was commanding the boy to tell him the truth.

Dexter pushed up his glasses with one of his hands and glanced away. It was obvious he didn't want to answer, which was quite ironic considering he was the one who wanted Eiko to talk to Christian about it. Unfortunately, she couldn't be glad about the turn of events. She was trapped on the bottom part of the staircase, watching an uncomfortable scene unfold. The moment Dexter glanced away, he accidentally locked his gaze with the girl's. That was enough of an indicator for Christian to look in their direction.

"What?!" He loudly asked, voice echoing throughout the mostly empty hallway. "What are *you* doin' here?"

Eiko's eyes were wide in fear. She felt like a wild trapped animal with no means of escape. Her flight or fight response had kicked in and her heartbeat was beating heavy against her ribcage. Even if she wanted to speak and come up with a lie on the spot, she couldn't think of anything no matter how hard she tried. Thankfully, Dexter spoke instead of her.

"It's none of your business," the cosplayer murmured, eyes narrowing down.

Christian looked amused as he took a step closer to the girl, making her take one backwards in reply. "You managed to lure lil' Eiko to your room?" He breathlessly laughed. "Wow, what a creep."

When the gamer opened her mouth to speak, no words came out. She felt dumb for even trying to do it in the first place. *So much for being lucky*, she sadly thought.

"Poor girl can't even defend herself. I didn't take you for the predator type, Dexter." He craned his neck so that he could give the boy a grin before turning to Eiko once again. He suddenly grabbed her by the wrist. His grip was tight and borderline painful – it made the girl want to instantly pull away. "Come on, Eiko. I'll save you from this stupid nerd."

The more she tried to struggle, the harder the grasp got. "Let go of me," Eiko weakly spoke, still trying to back away. Dexter instantly dropped the newspapers and roughly grabbed Christian by the shoulder, pulling him back. The action took the bully by surprise and he accidentally let go of the girl's wrist. Unfortunately for her, though, she had just tried to pull herself backwards. She realized her mistake far too late – Eiko stumbled backwards onto the stairs and fell down.

Everything went black.

Chapter 9

There was silence. Faint memories collided with
dreams and twisted into nightmares. There was
something bright coming from the corner – was it a
light? Eiko slowly opened her eyes, squinting at the
sunlight that hit her face. Its warmth was welcome
even if the sudden change of contrast was painful
for her pupils. As the girl regained her
consciousness, she felt a stabbing pain in her left
arm and the back of her head. She hissed in agony,
gritting her teeth in order to prevent herself from
making any loud noise. After maintaining her
composure, she finally gathered the strength and
motivation to glance around. She realized she was
laying on a soft but narrow bed in a room with
yellow walls. There was a small white-framed
window on her right that had translucent light blue
curtains. There was a faint smell of pills and
alcohol, and she realized she must have been in the
nurse's office.

What happened? Why am I here?

There were countless questions running through her
mind but she couldn't focus on any of them. Each
time she tried to stand up in order to look for the
nurse, the sharp pain manifested and she could only
lay back down onto the bed with a frustrated sigh.
Upon reaching for her face with her healthy hand,

the girl realized that her head had been bandaged. Her stomach twisted in anxiety; she opened her mouth to speak and slightly cringed at the lack of power her voice had. It was as if her vocal cords had completely given up. Eiko felt tears start to prickle in the corner of her eyes. She bit her bottom lip and moved her head as much as she could so that she could face the direction of the door. There was a figure dressed in white in the distance. It was a woman with a long gown; she had her hair up in a tight bun and looked more like a ghost than a human. She was sitting on a small wooden chair and was doing something on the desk. It didn't seem that she had noticed Eiko was awake.

The gamer knew that she had to speak in order to get her attention. She took a deep breath and ignored the way her lungs burned whenever she breathed. "E... Excuse... me..." she murmured, ignoring the way her dry throat hurt. Eiko realized she wasn't loud enough. She glared up at the ceiling and lightly shook her head. Instead of trying to speak again, though, she decided to do her best to stand up. Placing the healthy hand onto the mattress, Eiko cautiously pushed herself up into a sitting position. Her vision blacked out for a moment due to her blood pressure and she almost fell back down. Thankfully, she managed to keep her balance. After she managed to push herself up,

Eiko put one foot on the floor. She realized she wasn't wearing any shoes – the tiles were cold and uncomfortable. Upon looking down at herself, the girl saw that the rest of her clothes were intact.

Alright, almost there, she tried to motivate herself, *just need to stand up now. You can do this. You've got this.* Eiko slowly put her other foot on the tiles. With one last strong push made by her healthy arm, she successfully stood up. That was, of course, for mere moments. The moment she put her full weight on her feet, she fell forwards and landed on her knees, barely managing to protect herself from the fall with her hands. The bandaged wrist quietly popped and she felt as if her left side had been struck by lightning. The girl whined in pain – it seemed that the sound, combined with the force of her fall, was enough to finally get the nurse's attention. The ghostly woman straightened her back and swiftly turned around. She was tall, lean and young – Eiko thought she looked like Sister Ann, though she found out that they only resembled one another on the outside. The nurse was glaring at Eiko as if she had done something illegal as she got closer, hands firmly placed on her waist.

"What do you think you're doing?" The nurse loudly spoke as if she was a teacher scolding Eiko.

The girl glanced up from the floor. She couldn't

help but raise a brow. *Really? Is that what she's going to ask me?* "I fell," Eiko dumbly stated. There was no way she could give an answer to that question.

"That is why you're here in the first place, yes." The woman sighed, making her way over to the girl. She grabbed her by the upper part of her arm and pulled her up. Her grip was almost as painful as Christian's. Eiko couldn't believe how roughly she was being treated – wasn't she a patient? Shouldn't the medical staff be nice to people in pain? This was St Ambrose, after all. The staff wasn't exactly the best kind.

The girl couldn't hold her balance again. She fell down onto the bed and finally got let go. At least the bed itself was much better than the one on in her room. Despite it being on the smaller side, it was still much bigger and she didn't feel like she was about to fall each time she turned.

"Stay here," the nurse commanded, "I'll bring you water. If you try to stand up and end up falling again, I *won't* help you."

Eiko groaned in defeat. There wasn't anything other for her to do than to follow the command. Thankfully, the nurse didn't take long. She walked over to the bed less than a minute later and handed the girl a small glass of water. Eiko shakily grabbed it and slowly pulled it towards her lips. The taste of the beverage felt amazing considering she hadn't had anything to drink for a very long time. Her dry throat thanked her for finally doing something about and the gamer found out she could normally speak. Her vocal cords weren't torturing her anymore. "Thank you," Eiko mumbled out with a shy smile. The nurse had already turned her back and was in her usual position at the desk. The girl knew that, at least, this time she had certainly be loud enough to be heard. It didn't seem that the woman was interested in making friends, though. Despite wanting to fall back asleep and let her tired body rest, the curiosity kept Eiko's mind alive. She had to find out what happened – no matter how hard she tried to remember, she always got to a dead end.

"Uhm... Excuse me, may I ask what happened?" She tried to be as polite as possible, even if she clenched her teeth in anger when she got ignored yet again. Right as she was about to give up, there were three loud knocks on the door. Eiko instantly perked up. The nurse let out a heavy sigh before standing up from her desk and opening the door. There were two figures that sheepishly showed up and made their way inside. Despite squinting in order to help her bad eyesight, Eiko wasn't able to make out their face. She quietly groaned and started looking around for her glasses. Before she could find them neatly placed in the cupboard next to her, though, she heard her name being called out.

"Eiko!" Dexter exclaimed, trying to keep his voice quiet. "I'm so glad you're alright," he whined as he got to the girl and knelt in front of her bed. "Are you *really* alright?"

It was funny seeing the usually confident boy like that. Then again, Eiko couldn't make fun of him after realizing that the second figure was Christian. He was towering over Dexter and had his hands in the pocket of his pants. She couldn't see nor read his expression but something told her that he wasn't smiling. Eiko felt uncomfortable having him there but she didn't want to seem rude for asking him to leave – it couldn't be that bad, right? He wasn't bullying Dexter or anything. The girl's injury had somehow brought the two boys together for better or worse.

"Hey," Eiko quietly croaked, dry lips pursing into a smile. "I'm fine, don't worry." She slowly turned to the side, ignoring the pain in her head and wrist. "What happened?"

Dexter's eyebrows raised in confusion. He glanced back at Christian for a second who gave him a shrug for a reply. After turning back to Eiko, he lightly shook his head. "You… don't remember?"

The girl glanced away. "No... I only remember waking up here."

"Are you hurt?" Dexter worriedly asked.

"Of course she's hurt," Christian finally spoke, "she wouldn't be here if she wasn't."

Eiko flinched upon hearing the bully's voice. He was the last person she wanted to deal with at that very moment but unfortunately for her, fate had decided to play an ironic trick. She could only hope that he'd treat her better now that she was bedridden even if it would be for a little while.

"I'm sorry..." Christian mumbled out, eyes locked onto the floor. His teeth were grit and his fingers had formed fists – he looked like he was internally struggling. "It's all my fault. I shouldn't have tried to pull you. I... really am sorry."

Eiko's eyes widened in surprise. She instantly glanced up at the boy and felt at a complete loss of what to say and do. The apology was awkward even if it was genuine. The girl never knew how to act in these situations either way, except that now it was even more stressful. The guy who had been bullying her and her friend for all that time was suddenly apologizing? It made no sense!

I must have really hit my head.

"It's fine, I guess," Eiko murmured. "I mean… I didn't die so that's a plus?"

Dexter quietly chuckled. "Life has no extra lives."

Eiko instantly furrowed her brows. "That made no sense," she lightly scolded him even if she did laugh.

"How long are you going to be in here?" Christian butted in the conversation.

Both Dexter and Eiko became silent. The girl hated being in the center of attention yet it seemed that whatever happened, it always ended up with her playing the main role. Even if she didn't hate it, it didn't mean that she enjoyed falling down stairs, passing out and barely managing to avoid getting severely hurt. Then again… Things like that happened to everyone. Eiko knew she wasn't more special than the average person.

"I don't know," she sighed, "the nurse refuses to speak to me. I want to leave right now."

The cosplayer grinned. "Then let's do it!"

"Are you crazy?" Christian raised his voice. "She needs to stay here and rest until she feels better."

"You're not my mom." Eiko glared at the bully.

Christian gave out a loud sigh of frustration. "Whatever. I was just worried about you." His expression had twisted in sadness as he turned away without saying anything else and exited the door. He didn't even say goodbye to the nurse. It felt weird seeing him vulnerable, that much Eiko was sure of, though she wouldn't let him treat her however he wanted just so he could feel better. The girl made a mental note to start defending herself more in order to avoid such accidents. It didn't help that it was the bully who was the reason for her getting her, despite it being unintentional.

"What's up with him?" Dexter's voice took Eiko out of her thoughts.

She slightly raised her shoulders in reply. "I told you he's been acting weird."

"Well, whatever." The boy shook his head. "Do you want me to leave?"

Eiko sighed, "No, you can stay. I'll need some help getting up." She extended her arm for him to reach.

Dexter slightly backed away at first. He blinked once, then twice before taking a deep breath. "Alright." He smiled. "Hold my hand, I'll pull you up."

The girl did as she was told. She reached for him

with her healthy arm and wrapped her fingers around his wrist. The grip was weak, although it turned out to be just strong enough for her to successfully get on her feet. The blood rush to her legs make her lightheaded for a moment and she had to stay completely still until the darkness plaguing her vision faded away. Soon enough, though, she realized she could almost fully walk on her own. Eiko's lips had curled into a proud smile, one hand reaching for her glasses on the cupboard. After putting them on, she gave out a sigh of relief. *I can finally see again*, she thought.

"Put your arm around my shoulder," Dexter firmly spoke.

Eiko was taken by surprise at first. "Oh, you're finally deciding to play the hero?" She smugly commented.

The boy's cheeks flushed crimson. "I'm just trying to help you, sheesh. I'm partly responsible for your fall too."

"It's easier to just blame the bully." Eiko giggled, taking a step closer. She fulfilled his request to let him help her move. Even if she wouldn't ever admit it, she was thankful for his help. Each step kept becoming more and more painful and before they even reached the desk of the nurse, she felt like she was going to pass out. Her head was spinning – she felt like she was drunk, or at least what she assumed drunk people felt like.

"It's fine if Eiko leaves, right?" Dexter gently asked.

The nurse seemed even grumpier than before. She twisted her back so that she could take a look at the pair of them, eyeing them up and down. "You get only one visit here," she started, "if you get hurt again you'll have to take care of yourself."

Eiko and Dexter looked at each other. Neither of them knew what her answer meant. "Okay… Thank you." The girl bowed her head even if her expression showed the confusion she felt. Eiko had only one fear at that very moment and it was none other than Christian. A part of her was paranoid that he would've stayed outside and waited for them to head out, though she soon realized that wasn't the case. The mere thought of the bully made her feel anxious. Not only was he acting weird but he was trying to make it seem like he cared about her.

Just what exactly is he trying to accomplish?

"How's the walking," Dexter ly mumbled out.

The gamer nervously laughed. "It hurts a bit," she weakly replied, "but I'm going to be fine."

"You better be," he huffed.

Eiko couldn't help but feel amused. "You'd be a Paladin if this was a game. I can't imagine you being a Priest or Cleric."

"Paladin?" Dexter defensively spoke. His tone showed disappointment. "Pfft, please. I'd be a cool Warrior. I've always wanted to cosplay as one."

"Nope," Eiko said, "you're far too nice and supportive."

Despite feeling embarrassed, Dexter ended up agreeing with her. "Fine, fine. What are you then?"

"I usually play as a caster. Sometimes I'm a Mage while other times I'm a Necromancer," Eiko hummed.

"Necromancer?" The boy's face paled. "I think I'd rather have you as a Mage."

The girl smirked. That was the usual reaction she got when people found out she enjoyed playing as a Necromancer. They kept telling her that she didn't fit the edgy stereotype and looked far too innocent to be playing such an evil class. Eiko enjoyed summoning undead armies far too much to give up on the role, which is why she often ended up being one. Mages were fun and smart but Necromancers were stylish and cool. "We should definitely play sometimes."

"What do you mean?" Dexter looked at her.

"Oh yeah! I brought some of my tabletop games here." Eiko perked up in happiness. "I was thinking we could play them in the library but... I don't think that'll be such a great idea."

The boy chuckled. "I don't think I've played anything like that before. I'm more of a video game type of guy."

"Well, there's a first time for everything. Would you like to play with me?" The girl's voice was hopeful.

Dexter's lips curled into a smile. "Of course. You'll need to teach me everything but I promise I'm a fast learner."

"Great!" Eiko exclaimed. "Let's start today!"

The cosplayer raised a brow in suspicion. "Today?" He asked. "You can barely walk, Eiko. You need to rest." He stopped himself for a moment, thinking of his words. "I don't want to act like your mother but it's obvious you're hurt. Your head and hand are bandaged."

"You'll heal me," Eiko replied. Her shoulders slouched in defeat. "I know, I know. I promise I'll rest." She glanced up at the girls' dorms. Thankfully, Kate wasn't anywhere around and

Christian had vanished out of sight. Due to thinking about her favorite RPGs, Eiko forgot about the blatant pain in her head. When she got back to reality, she grinded her teeth in order to keep herself from making any sounds of pain and further worrying Dexter. He had helped her so much, he didn't deserve to feel anxious. "Thanks for the help," she murmured.

"I'm not letting you go just yet," Dexter quickly added, "you'll need help with the stairs."

Eiko's stomach turned in nervousness. She didn't want to remind him of what happened the last time they got in the same dorm together – she was pretty sure it would be hard to forget. His idea wasn't that surprising considering the fact that she could barely walk on her own. It was a sad turn of fate for her to be trapped on the top floor. At least she didn't hear the noise from the campus while the students talked with each other.

"Alright," she sighed, "just be quick about it."

Dexter nodded. He tightened his grip around her waist and led them to the front door. Eiko couldn't help but anxiously glance around in worry, eyes wide in fear as she expected the worst to happen. She was absolutely sure Kate would suddenly show up and start spreading rumors about them – she seemed to be that type of person. Thankfully, her negative thoughts didn't turn out to be true. The long climb up the stairs was as calm as it was painful. The girl's head pulsated with each step she took, though the relief she felt when they got to her room unscathed overwhelmed the pain.

"Wow," Dexter started, "didn't know you lived so high up."

Eiko gave a shrug of her shoulders. "It was the only room left," she replied, "I don't mind it at all. This way I can be completely alone most of the time."

"I'm kind of jealous." The boy looked amazed. "I mean… I could certainly have it worse. The third floor isn't that bad but you'll never guess *who* lives on top and likes working out at 12am." He rolled his eyes.

The girl lightly shook her head with a smile. *Of course it would be Christian. Life is always unfair like that,* she thought, going through the uniform's pockets in order to take her key out. When she did, she moved away from Dexter and leaned against the wall in order to be able to manage her own weight before unlocking the door. After she was done, she turned around. "Thanks," she said, "I really appreciate it."

Dexter ruffled the back of his head, returning the friendly smile. "Hey, it was no big deal, really. I'm glad to have helped," he stated, "you have no idea how much I freaked out when you fell."

"It must have been scary…" Eiko's cheerful expression morphed into sadness. She looked down. "I'm sorry."

"Sorry?" Dexter tilted his head to the side in confusion. "It's not your fault, Eiko. I was the one who made you come with me. If anything, I should be the one apologizing."

The girl glanced back at him. "No one got severely hurt. Did you at least go through the newspapers?"

"No way," Dexter quickly replied, "I couldn't just sit there while you were unconscious. Your wellbeing is the most important. We can look through them whenever, the library is always open."

"I guess…" Eiko trailed off. She didn't want Dexter to get punished but it was obvious that he didn't want to find out any vital information without her being there. She still couldn't understand why he was so adamant on finding the school's dark secrets – she was pretty sure there would be a lot of them. St Ambrose looked extremely suspicious, though that didn't meant they could risk their lives in order to find out everything. "I'll go get some rest now," she mumbled out, "thanks again."

Without waiting for the boy's reply, Eiko limped inside and closed the door behind her. She didn't bother locking it since she knew no one cared enough to try and break into her room. Even if walking was still as difficult as ever, she felt much better. The exhaustion she felt from the countless stairs had almost fully faded away and she could keep her balance for more than five seconds. The annoying headache was still present, though it wasn't as strong as before. Then again, she still didn't waste any time grabbing her phone and plopping onto the bed with a loud thud. She didn't bother pulling the covers up since she knew she wouldn't be sleeping any time soon even if it was becoming dark. Dinner time would be skipped, that much she was sure of due to her lack of appetite and her desire to catch up on her daily quests. Needless to say, Eiko spent the rest of the night playing on her phone. Even after the device's battery died, she plugged it in again and sat on the desk in order to continue. Perhaps it wasn't the best idea since her head and eyes started hurting again, though she couldn't care about that. She finally felt at peace and happy.

Eiko never understood people who looked down on video games. It seemed that St Ambrose had a strong case of the anti-technology. Most religious schools weren't big on tech stuff though she never believed it would be so bad. It was almost as if all the staff members were brainwashed into thinking that phones and computers were some greater evil that was out to get them.

Do they really believe they're helping us by not letting us use anything? Eiko narrowed her eyes, trying to focus onto the small screen. Her thumbs were quickly tapping over it. *It just doesn't make any sense. I've never heard of a school doing something like this before. Maybe something really is going on... Maybe Dexter is right.*

There was a quiet sigh of frustration that could be heard. Eiko accidentally died. Her whole body kept becoming more exhausted by the moment and her usually cat like reflexes had slowed down. The girl glanced up at the ceiling as she leaned back on the wooden chair, hands still holding the burning device. There was no point in her continuing – her phone felt like it was about to explode any second now and she was far too tired to be able to concentrate. Even if the girl had slept in that morning, she still managed to swiftly fall asleep, much to her surprise.

Chapter 10

The next few days were spent in recovery. Eiko was allowed to skip school once in order to rest. By the time she removed the bandages from her head and hand, she felt much better even if she was still slightly lightheaded due to lack of food – Eiko's appetite had gone downhill ever since she got injured. That didn't stop Dexter from sneaking out food during lunch and dinner time. He always brought her vanilla muffins. Even if the girl kept telling him that she didn't want any food, she still accepted the sentimental gifts and ended up eating them later during the day. She had a weak spot for sweet stuff, after all, and Dexter kept abusing it.

Before she knew it, things were back to normal. She kept running from class to class, tightly clutching her bag in order to avoid having any of her books falling out of it. The fear of being late and being punished was omnipresent, even if her friend kept giving her weird looks about it. Eiko always got annoyed when he downplayed the punishments – she wasn't used to being physically hurt, which is why it was very stressful for her. By the time the first exam came, Eiko had managed to learn everything by heart. Even if she was never that interested in maintaining good grades, the anxiety born from the possibility of failure always made her study extremely hard weeks before the actual exam.

This always ended up with her acing everything that came her way, much to Dexter's annoyance who was still struggling with bad grades. Each time Eiko proposed to help him, though, he always denied her. The girl wasn't sure whether he simply wasn't interested in maintaining good grades, other than those he received in math class, or he was internally struggling with his pride. Then again, there wasn't much she could do about it if he wouldn't let her, which is why she let the subject go and instead focused on St Ambrose and its secrets.

After a particularly difficult pop quiz, the duo had found themselves in Dexter's room; Eiko wasn't afraid of being seen with him anymore since it turned out that the other students, other than Christian and Kate time from time, completely ignored their existence. The boy had managed to keep the papers for much longer after sweet-talking his way into the librarian's approval.

"You mean to tell me that you didn't go through even one paper all this time?" Eiko incredulously asked. Both of them had sat on the floor with the newspapers scattered around them.

"I mean…" Dexter cleared his throat. "I did go through one or two but I got bored from reading so much boring stuff."

Eiko giggled. "Everything is boring if it's not math

or conspiracy theories, huh?"

The boy proudly pushed his chest out as he put his hands on his hips, lips curling into a grin. "Of course!"

"Alright, alright." The gamer defensively held out her hands. "Let's get this over with before dinner time. I'm hungry for once."

Despite the pair's endless motivation at first, it ended up fading away less than two hours later. There were just so many newspapers and none of them seemed to have any important information. It was as if they were reading boring text books except that they weren't learning anything that would help them further down the line. The pile on the side of the room kept becoming bigger. Eiko was the first one to take a break – she went into the bathroom to wash her face with cold water in order to wake herself up. She could barely keep her eyes open from the boredom. By the time she came back, Dexter had pulled out a vanilla muffin. The blatant sleepiness instantly disappeared as Eiko dug into the sweetness. The sugar rush she got kept her awake the next hour.

"There's nothing here!"

Now it was Dexter's turn to whine and give up. He threw the newspaper he was holding onto the floor and leaned back, holding his weight with his hands. His legs were crossed.

The sudden loud exclamation startled Eiko. She lightly jumped and looked up. "We're almost done," she softly spoke.

"That's the problem," Dexter sighed, "we spent all this time, read through all this boring stuff and found absolutely nothing."

"It makes sense that they wouldn't make any bad news available to the students..." Eiko mumbled out, gently placing the newspaper on the ground. "They wouldn't want to make St Ambrose look back."

The boy quietly hummed. "So you think they're hiding it?"

"I'm pretty sure they are." Eiko nodded. "But why would Christian, of all people, be the one with the information?"

Dexter glanced away, putting his hand on his chin. He kept silent for a moment, the cogs in his mind twisting and turning, trying to think of a possibility. "Maybe he stumbled across it by accident."

"By accident?" The girl dumbly repeated.

"It's certainly possible. Maybe he was too afraid of

showing it to anyone since he thought he'd get in trouble so he just… Tried to throw it into the trash." The cosplayer shrugged. "This brings us back to the first idea I had – you need to talk to him to find out what he knows."

Eiko groaned in frustration. "Why me?" She folded her arms across her chest. "Why can't *you* do it instead?"

"I'm pretty sure he'll punch my lights out if I go anywhere near him, especially after he got the blame for your fall." Dexter chuckled.

Eiko looked down. "Ugh, fine," she murmured, "I'll do it. But you'll owe me big time for what I'm about to put myself through." She perked up and pointed with her index finger. Just like Dexter, she didn't want to anywhere near the bully but it looked like she didn't have any other choice. Maybe he would treat her better for once now that he felt guilty for hurting her.

"Good luck," Dexter said.

"Yeah, I'll need it," Eiko replied.

Chapter 11

Finding Christian was an easy enough task, though managing to hold a conversation for longer than a few seconds proved to be difficult. Unlike the beginning when Eiko first started going to St Ambrose, he was now avoiding her as if she was the plague. Each time she got closer, he backed away and instead turned to his friends. The girl was far too shy to interrupt their conversation and end up being the center of attention once more, which is why she gave up. It was an interesting experience – the bullied never searched for their bullies and yet there Eiko was, searching for the boy who tried to ruin her life the moment she stepped inside the campus. She was still mad at him for taking her phone without her permission and letting her fall but there were more important things to worry about. If Dexter was right, and she hoped that he wasn't, then St Ambrose was covering up something evil. Sometimes sacrifices had to be made for the greater good.

It wasn't until she stood in front of the door after Biology class ended that he finally gave her the needed response. At first he tried to push her away but when he realized she wouldn't move, he took a step backwards and glared daggers into her eyes. Thankfully, the teacher and most of the students were gone, leaving Eiko to her own devices and methods.

"What the hell do you want? *Move*." Christian roughly commanded even if his voice was weaker than it had been before. He wasn't threatening enough.

Eiko's voice was quiet and gentle as if she was smothering a child. "We need to talk, Christian."

"No, we don't. Now move before I make you," he snapped.

"It's not about me getting hurt." The girl took a deep breath. "It's something else – something important. Please, we need to talk."

Christian's eyes widened in surprise. He opened his mouth to speak, though no words came out at first. After shaking his head in order to gather his thoughts, he gave out a loud sigh of defeat and sat on the desk closest to the door. Despite him showing signs of cooperation, his features were still twisted in the familiar grimace. "What's it about then?"

"Can we… Maybe talk about it outside?" Eiko glanced behind her for a moment. "I'm afraid someone will enter."

Even if Christian raised a brow, he still quickly stood up from the desk. The girl finally moved away from the door and led him outside; they walked in complete and awkward silence. Eiko's eyes were glued to the ground and she tried to contain her nervousness. She didn't like being alone with Christian – she didn't feel safe. She could feel the looks of confusion the other students gave her and the boy as they walked past them and that only made her negative feelings stronger. To her relief, though, their pace was swift and they ended up outside the main school building less than a minute later. Eiko slowly breathed out and leaned against a wall to the side. Christian had found himself in front of his, giving her a skeptical look with his hands folded across his chest.

"Get on with it already," he mumbled out.

"Right," Eiko started, "right, yeah. Uhm..." She looked to the side, fingers tightly clutching the strap of her bag. "Okay so… Dexter and I think that there's something going on here in St Ambrose," she quietly spoke, "but we don't know how to prove it."

Christian breathlessly laughed. "Dexter, huh? I knew it was a mistake giving you a chance." He turned around and started walking away.

"Please!" Eiko suddenly exclaimed, wrapping her fingers around his wrist in order to prevent him from leaving. "Please, you need to listen. I don't know who else to tell this to."

The bully twisted his neck in order to glance behind him. His eyes were even wider than before, though he still roughly pulled away from the girl's weak grip. Eiko ended up stumbling forwards from the strong force and bumped into him. She put her hands on his back in order to protect herself from the possible fall. That was when Christian fully turned around. The gamer was surprised to see his flushed cheeks as she backed away and tried to maintain her composure. She looked up at him again with a pleading expression.

"Fine," Christian groggily replied, running a hand through his hair before he slightly backed away. "Just… Get it over with."

It felt weird seeing him so embarrassed and as much as Eiko wanted to comment on it and make him feel even shier, she decided that it wasn't the right time. After all, she had worked so hard just to grab his attention for a few minutes – she couldn't ruin this chance no matter what happened. "Well, as I said, there's something going on here. I… I'm not sure what it is but I know it's bad." Eiko studied the boy's expression for any sort of reaction; her goal was to make him confess knowing vital information. Unfortunately for her, he was completely unreadable. The embarrassment had fully faded away and he was looking at her as if she was a teacher explaining a boring lesson.

"I don't know how to say this without making you mad…" Eiko trailed off, biting her bottom lip.

Christian took a step closer. "What is it? You can tell me – we've come so far already."

Once again, Eiko found herself at a crossroad. She could either tell him the truth about her and Dexter sneaking into his room in order to get her phone back or she could protect her friend and place all the blame on herself. There was always the option of lying, though she had found herself at a dead end in that scenario; she couldn't think of any realistic lie that wouldn't raise the bully's suspicion. There was only one thing left for her to do.

"Remember when you got my phone?" She weakly asked.

Christian looked confused. "Yeah. What about it?"

"Well…" Eiko glanced away. "I kind of snuck into your room in order to get it back."

"You *what*?!" Christian suddenly raised his voice. His mouth was open in disbelief and his brows were set up high. His blue eyes looked even brighter than usual.

Eiko was quick to defensively raise her hands. "I—I didn't touch anything. I just got my phone back and went on with my day. I swear on my life."

"… How did you even get inside?" The boy had managed to control himself from over reacting even if that didn't mean he felt comfortable with the situation. His cheeks were starting to redden up again.

"It's a long story." The girl ly waved her hand, lips curling into a sheepish smile. "A—Anyway, that's not the important information I wanted to tell you."

Christian held his head in his hands and walked around in circles in disbelief. "I can't believe this," he whispered, "you got into my room."

Eiko quietly sighed. It wasn't her intention to stray off the conversation at hand but there wasn't anything she could do about it now without the possibility of alienating Christian further. She had practically confessed to sneaking in his dorm without permission and going through his belongings – she would react the same way if someone else came up and told her the same thing. She couldn't blame him. "My phone is extremely important to me," she murmured, gently placing her hand on the boy's shoulder. It seemed that the action was enough to make him stop moving. "I just had to get it back no matter what."

"You didn't have to break into my room," Christian replied. His voice was shaky but quiet.

Eiko's shoulders slouched in defeat. "Can I please ask you something?"

"No." He shook his head. "I don't even know what to think about you anymore."

"What do you mean?" The girl asked in disbelief. "You're the one who practically stole my phone away from me even after I told you 'no' at least five times. Stop acting like you're the victim here and let me say what I brought you here for!"

The sudden outburst of anger made the bully stiffen. Eiko blinked a few times before realizing what she had done. She covered her mouth with her hand and kept glancing around in order to find out whether raising her voice had brought any unwanted attention towards them. Thankfully, her suspicions were proven wrong. Most students were slowly walking around and talking with each other – they didn't care about Christin and Eiko since they knew he was most likely bullying her at that very moment.

"I found a piece of a newspaper article inside your bin," she continued, voice quiet and cautious, "it was about the Principal being accused of doing something. Do you know where the rest of it is?"

Christian's face paled. "Oh... *that*." He nervously ruffled the back of his head. "I don't know."

Eiko's shoulders slouched in defeat. This wasn't the answer she was expecting. What would he even win by keeping information like that? It didn't make any sense for him to protect St Ambrose. "Please, Christian, you need to tell me the truth. Don't tell me you like the way we're being treated by the staff. They're awful."

"It's none of your business." The bully's tone was cold. "I'm done talking about this."

Before Eiko had a chance to hold onto him in order to prevent him from walking away like she had done before, Christian was already out of her sight. He was quick on his feet as he half-jogged away and wildly waved to his group of friends who were waiting for him in front of the main gate. Eiko sunk down until she sat on the rough ground and pulled her knees up to her chest, wrapping her hands around them so that she could hold them close. *Damn it*, she thought, biting the inside of her cheek, *so much for that... At least now I know that Christian has some information.* She stood completely still, mindlessly staring off into the distance. Even as the weather kept becoming colder and the sky became darker as the last rays of sunlight disappeared behind the gray clothes, Eiko

144

didn't move from her position.

Most students went back to their dorms so that they could rest before dinner time. The whole campus became quiet – the only sounds that could be heard were from the strong gust of wind and dead leaves that were scattered around and kept being pushed in different directions. It was relaxing in a way, though it wasn't calming enough to soothe Eiko's anxiety. All her efforts had turned out to be in vain, after all. She knew it would most likely be impossible to make the boy talk to her again especially after what she said. The gamer should have lied in order to not make him mad, she realized, though it was far too late. *If only I could turn back time and fix my past mistakes…* Eiko lightly shook her head. Now wasn't the time to think about what-ifs and could-have-beens. She had to come up with a new plan in order to get Christian's attention and make him find out that she and Dexter were on his side. They wanted to fight against St Ambrose's strict and unfair rules. They wanted to find out the truth.

I need to do something – anything – to make Christian talk. Dexter was right all along. There is something going on here after all but… Is it really our job to make things right? I guess I have no other choice. It's far too late to back down now.

Meeting with Dexter certainly wasn't the most pleasurable experience. Eiko felt ashamed because of her outburst of confidence that turned out to be fruitless. Much to her surprise, though, Dexter didn't scold her.

"It's fine, Eiko," he said. "This isn't anything to be frustrated over. We've got the rest of the school year to find out the truth."

The girl shook her head, trying to fight off tears of anger that burned the corners of her eyes. "You got in trouble so many times for me and I can't do even one thing right!"

Dexter defensively raised his hands as if he was protecting himself from the sudden aggression born in Eiko's tone. When she realized that he was scared, she instantly backed away and bowed in apology. "It wasn't a big deal, really." He breathlessly chuckled. "I had fun and that's what matters."

"But... But we still need to find what this school has done," Eiko whined.

"The Principal, not the school." Dexter was quick to correct her. "We can't assume everyone here is guilty. We don't even know whether the article was a lie or not."

Eiko glanced at the ground, teeth firmly clenched in frustration. "You should've seen Christian's reaction. He was super defensive and instantly snapped at me. He knew he'd get in trouble if he shared anything."

"Do you think he actually has the rest of the article?" Dexter tilted his head in question.

The girl replied with a weak shrug of her shoulders. "Maybe, maybe not. We can't know for certain…" She looked up, gaze now locked with Dexter's. "What do you think we should do?"

"We should wait," he replied.

Eiko opened her mouth to speak although no words came out at first. She was confused. "What—What do you mean by 'wait'? We don't have enough time."

Dexter sighed. "Now that Christian knows that we know about him sneaking around the school trying to uncover secrets, he's going to be even more careful."

"This is why we need to let him know that we're on his side before he completely shuts us off," she firmly stated.

"We'll just end up making him feel even weirder about the whole situation," Dexter groaned, "he's definitely going to think that we're trying to get him in trouble because he bullied us."

Eiko gasped. "I can't believe you're still thinking about that. He helped us!"

"Us?" The boy rolled his eyes and clicked his tongue before pointing at Eiko with his index finger. "He helped *you*."

"Oh, please." Eiko folded her arms across her chest. "He hasn't bullied you since the accident, right? That's better than nothing."

Dexter stood up from the bench and glared at the girl. He was still a bit taller than her, though she managed to stand her ground. "You don't know anything about what I've been through!"

"We've both been through *enough* together. Why can't you trust me?" The gamer asked, as he lowered his gaze in sadness.

"Why can't you trust *me*?" Dexter instantly replied.

Eiko couldn't believe what she was hearing – the disbelief was clear across her features. "You—You were the one who proposed to try to find out more information! I don't understand you at all..."

"I know you don't," he sighed, "I was an idiot for thinking otherwise."

There was heavy silence that followed. Eiko's brows were furrowed and lips were sealed; she had found herself at a complete loss of what to do and say. She never expected to get in a fight with Dexter, especially after everything that happened. It was obvious they both needed to stay with each other in order to support one another but... It seemed that things had changed. Eiko could only watch as her friend turned his back on her and swiftly made his way back to the dorm. The worst part of it all was that she didn't even know what she had done wrong – she only wanted to help him reach his goal because he helped get her phone back. It was an act of kindness that was supposed to be returned later down the line.

"Great," Eiko mumbled out, blowing air upwards at her bangs. Her hair flew for a moment before falling flat against her forehead. "Now both of them are mad at me."

There was a cold gust of wind that made a shiver run down her spine. She wrapped her hands around her opposite arms and, with her head hung low, decided to head back to her room. There wasn't much the gamer could do at that very moment, especially after accidentally ruining anything. She hated being the source of problems and as much as she tried to avoid getting in trouble, it seemed that trouble itself followed along everywhere she went after starting school. It was an agonizing twist of fate she didn't exactly know how to deal with considering she used to be the quiet shy kid in class. Now, she was stuck on a crossroad leading towards different paths. Eiko couldn't help but wonder what option she would choose if she was playing a visual novel game.

There was the possibility of her heading back to Dexter's place and apologizing, although she didn't think of herself as guilty in the situation. If anything, he was the guilty one. Each time she thought of her friend, her blood boiled. No, she couldn't confront him about what happened yet. The wound was still fresh and pouring salt into it wouldn't heal it.

The second option was seeking Sister Anne's help. She seemed nice and trustworthy, though that didn't change the fact that she was still part of the school's staff and could turn evil at any given moment. Not only that, but Eiko would feel even worse if the sister got into even more trouble because of her. She didn't want to be the cause for her unemployment.

The last option was the worst – Eiko could confront Christian. Even if they had fought with each other less than ten minutes ago, she didn't feel anything. After all, they weren't close nor were they friends. They used to be a victim and a bully and now they were… Eiko really wasn't sure what they were but it certainly was better than being mad at one another over something dumb.

"Okay," she breathed out, "okay… I guess there's no other choice."

"Look at this weirdo talking to herself. Ugh, pathetic."

Kate's familiar voice sounded behind Eiko and before she could fall into the obvious trap laid out for her from the evil genius that was the plastic girl, Eiko half-jogged up the stairs while being careful not to fall. The last thing she wanted was to get hurt the same way again. This time there wouldn't be any Dexter or Christian to save her and she was pretty sure Kate would just leave her on the floor to die if she had the chance.

Despite the small room, the girl felt at peace when she reached her own sanctuary. There were still countless anxious thoughts running through her tortured mind but at least she could be safe from the rest of the bullies. Then again, she was sure she'd have to confront the biggest bully of them all sooner or later. Despite not wanting to make Christian even more frustrated with her, Eiko knew she had to be strong in order to deal with the consequences. She was sure that this wasn't a situation that could be left along for too long before things started getting bad – if there was anything suspicious happening in St Ambrose, then they had to find out about it as soon as possible. The best thing she could do right then was to win Christian's trust in order to make him share vital information. Of course, Eiko knew that would be easier said than done, considering she had currently found herself stuck between a rock and a stone. She shook her head in a vain attempt to take control over her emotions and moved away from the front door. The girl couldn't help but give a loving glance to her phone and the few games she had brought with her, though that was no time to relax. She couldn't aimlessly linger for long in case things got worse.

This is why with newborn confidence, she ran a hand through her hair and opened the front door once again, adamant on finding Christian and making him listen to what she had to say. Unfortunately for her, she hadn't realized that less than a minute had passed and Kate and her friends we still happily chatting away on the stairs. Eiko's stomach sunk in fear and she felt even worse than before. Kate was the last person who needed to know what was going on and yet there she was, preventing Eiko from freely moving along without having to pass by her judgmental stare. The gamer had to take a few deep breaths in order to compose herself and she started going down the stairs as quiet as she could – she felt like a mouse trying to pass through a pride of starving lions. Of course, just as the wildlife, Eiko was stopped by Kate.

"What're you doing pacing around?" The bully clicked her tongue.

The girl gave out a quiet sigh of exhaustion. "Please, Kate, I'm in a hurry."

"*I'm in a hurry!*" Kate sarcastically replied, doing her best to imitate Eiko's tone in a not so flattering manner. The rest of the girls loudly chuckled, their voices echoing throughout the building.

There was the familiar ting of frustration that flowed through the girl's veins, though she gnashed her teeth and tried to keep herself calm. After all, losing her cool was what the bullies wanted and she didn't want to give them anything that would make them happy. "Can you just please late me go?"

"You keep saying 'please' so much." Kate rolled her eyes. "Honestly, it's annoying as hell. Do you know that such special words lose their meaning after being used over and over again?"

Eiko furrowed her brows in confusion. "That doesn't make any sense—"

There was suddenly a finger brought to her lips, followed by a loud hush. "Shush, now." Kate

grinned. "In order for you to make it up to us...
How about, let's say, you do our homework for the
next month?"

The two girls giggled behind Kate.

"What?" Eiko accidentally raised her voice. "I
haven't even done anything--"

The annoying finger tapped against her lips again,
making her back off. The gamer's eyes narrowed
down to a glare.

"I told you to shush." Kate returned the glare of
hatred, though her lips were still curled into a
victorious smirk. "You wouldn't want to wake up
your classmates now, would you? You've been here
for less than a month and you're already trying to
make everyone hate you."

The wheels in Eiko's mind twisted and turned, and
she found herself completely ignoring the awful
insults leaving Kate's mouth. No matter how much
she thought about the current situation, though,
Eiko realized that there was no way for her to
escape other than to accept the unfair proposal that
was more of a command than anything. She still had
a hard time processing that bullying was such a big
problem in St Ambrose, but the best thing she could
do was to roll with it for as long as she could.

"Fine," Eiko growled, "I'll do your stupid homework."

Kate's glare instantly disappeared. The smile she carried no longer had any hidden menacing feelings behind it as she clasped her hands together and moved to the side in order to make way for Eiko to depart. "Wonderful! I knew we'd be able to come to an agreement."

Eiko wanted to laugh in her face. The plastic girl was acting as if they had made some sort of deal that would benefit the both of them. Charisma truly was a powerful weapon.

Even though the gamer managed to leave the group of bullies mostly unscathed, except for the empty promise she made that she was sure would come back around, she knew that the hardest part had yet to come. There was a an awful feeling of dread deep in her gut that wouldn't go away no matter how hard she tried to fight it off. It was as if the more she focused on being calm, the more anxious she got. This is why instead of over thinking each and every possible scenario of what would happen when she met with Christian again, she decided to just get it over with before she lost the little courage she had.

Unfortunately for her, though, the campus was starting to get empty. There were a few students here and there but most of them seemed like the nerdy quiet types that would shiver if someone of bigger size passed by. There were no bullies around, nor were there troublemakers like Eiko and Dexter. When the thought of her friend passed through her mind again, she shook her head and took in a deep breath. Eiko had to remind herself that the reason she was trying to find Christian was because Dexter was mad at her even though she hadn't done anything wrong. With a tired sigh, Eiko's narrowed eyes scanned the rest of the yard leading to the entrance. There was no sign of her target, much to her annoyance. She knew she had to head over to the boys' dorm unseen so that she could freely grab Christian's attention.

The gamer stood completely still for a moment as she cautiously glanced around, afraid that she was acting too suspiciously. Thankfully, the few students that were left didn't seem to notice her at all – this gave her a free pass all the way to the opposite building. That was where she saw a group of four boys happily chatting with each other, each of them holding a different colored notebook. Eiko tried to make it look like it was mere coincidence she was so close to the boys' dorm and in order to look more natural, she leaned against the brick wall and tried to pull her phone out.

'*Tried*' being the key word.

Poor Eiko still wasn't used to the awful No-Fun-Allowed rule that seemed to plague the entirety of St Ambrose. She ended up looking at her nails just to have something to do, and made a mental note to make them shorter the next chance she had. By the time she was done going through each and every nail, the faint voices of the group of boys disappeared into the distance. Now, Eiko found herself staring at the front door leading to the long staircase and occupied rooms. It was weird, to say the least. All previous visits to the boys' dorm had been with someone else, which is why she didn't remember feeling so worried. The adrenaline was pumping through her veins and she was ready to fight off anyone who stood in her way, despite not wanting to get in trouble.

Much to the girl's surprise, though, the dorm was just as empty as the exterior of the campus. There were no plastics to be afraid of and she was sure Dexter was in his room, which is why there was a sudden burst of confidence that ran through her body. She took one step towards the staircase. The sound her shoe made was much louder than she would've liked, though it certainly wasn't loud enough to catch anyone's attention. This is why Eiko continued walking while sparing a glance behind her every so often just to make sure there wasn't anyone being stealthy like her. By the time she reached the door leading to Christian's room, she was lightly panting and could feel a slight burn in her thighs. The feeling of exhaustion soon faded away and she was left staring at the nameplate on the door.

"Oh man…" Eiko mumbled out, running a hand through her hair. There was a nervous smile spread across her pale features. "What am I even doing?"

This wasn't the way things were supposed to happen – she never believed that St Ambrose would feel so *off* and she definitely hadn't expected to be confronting someone who bullied her so that she could show him that she was on his side when it came to finding out the secrets of the school. It all seemed like a mystery video game for her. Then again, she was quite good at those types of games.

Eiko knocked three times. Her knuckles lightly grazed the door.

There was no response.

She knocked two more times. There was more force in the action.

The more she waited, though, the more frustrated she got. There was still no response and she couldn't hear any sort of movement from behind the door. With jaw firmly locked in place, Eiko tried to knock one last time before giving up. She thought, "I need to relax or I'm going to break my teeth." There was a loud creak that echoed off the walls of the dorm and the door got opened before she could place her fist against it. The gamer slightly stumbled forwards but was quick to step back in order to keep a safe distance between her and Christian.

"What the hell are you doing here?" He rudely asked even if his statement held no malice. There was no frustration in his voice and the only thing the girl could detect was exhaustion. What reason would Christian, of all people, have to be tired?

Eiko sighed, glancing at the ground. "I'm sorry about earlier," she said. "What I did wasn't cool. I shouldn't have made you feel uncomfortable."

Christian couldn't help but tilt his head to the side in confusion. It was obvious he hadn't expected Eiko to say that. Nonetheless, his cold and quiet persona overtook the situation once more. "It doesn't really matter. I don't care," he mumbled out, "now if you're done…" His voice trailed off as he slowly started closing the door.

The gamer almost missed her chance but, thankfully, she managed to put her leg in between the doorframe and successfully prevented Christian from closing it. "Wait," she pleaded. "Let's talk. I promise I won't ask you anything you don't want to answer. Could you just let me in, please?"

There was silence that followed. For a moment Eiko thought that he was going to push her away and slam the door in her face, though he surprised her once again.

"Sure, whatever." He rolled his eyes.

Eiko couldn't control the way her lips curled into a smile of happiness. Considering everything bad that had happened, she hadn't expected to be victorious right then and there. She certainly wasn't going to start complaining. Without wasting any time, she took off her shoes and entered the small familiar room. When she passed the bin next to the door, she gave it one quick glance in order to see whether there was anything there but she ended up being disappointed. There wasn't any sort of clue – there were only empty packets and cans of fast food and soda.

"So, what did you want to talk about?" Christian's voice took her out of her thoughts and she stiffened in surprise. The victorious smile she wore turned into one of nervousness as she slowly and cautiously made her way through the short corridor.

By the time she entered the main room, the bully had already sat on the chair in front of the desk, facing her. Eiko looked at the bed for a moment before lightly shaking her head. She didn't want to try and make herself feel at home because she still didn't know whether Christian would snap at her again or not. The gamer awkwardly leaned against the doorframe and tried to make it seem like she was relaxed.

"I just wanted you to know that I'm your side," she said.

Christian raised a brow. "What side?"

"You know..." She trailed off and glanced away. "The whole thing about the article exposing our Principal."

The bully suddenly stood up from the chair. Eiko quickly held her hands in front of herself in a defensive motion. "Wait, Christian! I won't tell anyone, I swear. I want to solve this case as much as you do, trust me."

"Why should I trust you?" He growled, hands forming fists.

The gamer glanced at him. "Because we're all suffering here," she murmured, eyes narrowing down in sadness. Her arms were now calmly resting at her sides. "No one likes this school – not even the staff members. I'm sure Kate and her groupies have their own problems as well. Neither of us want to be here."

"Boo-hoo, that's really sad," Christian sarcastically spoke, "I hate people who play the victim all the time."

Eiko couldn't help but raise a brow in suspicion. It was quite hypocritical of him to say that considering he was the reason there were so many bullied victims around, but she decided not to press the matter further and instead focused on what was important. "We might be victims but that doesn't mean we can't change our future. If we just work together…"

"Then what?" He loudly asked. "Nothing is going to change if we get along."

"But if we found out what the Principal has done then we could bring some clarity," Eiko defended herself.

Christian gave out a loud sigh of frustration. "I can't believe you're still thinking about that. You really are hopeless."

"If you didn't think the same way I did then…" She motioned for the bin. "How did you even get your hands on the piece of paper? You can't just stumble across something like that – you must've gotten it from somewhere."

"I told you already, it's none of your business," he firmly stated.

Eiko placed her hand on her chest and took a step forwards. "It *is* my business. The students of St Ambrose deserve to know the truth no matter how painful it might be."

"There's no big truth that'll make this school worse than it already is."

The girl's brows furrowed in sadness. "I'm not trying to make it worse... I'm trying to make it better."

Christian found himself at a loss of words. His eyes were wide in surprise and his lips were slightly parted, though no sound escaped them. He suddenly glanced at the ground before sitting back on the chair and running a hand through his short black hair. It was obvious he was having a hard time winning the debate. He placed his elbow onto the desk and held the side of his head with his hand. There was a breathless chuckle that followed as he shook his head in disbelief.

This was the first time the gamer realized that the window had been open all that time. The air inside the room was chilly and she couldn't stop the shiver of coldness that ran through her body. Even if his room was on a much lower floor than hers, it was somehow colder than her own. Nonetheless, she stood her ground. She finally had the upper hand and wouldn't let the slim chance slip away. She couldn't believe that Christian had turned out to be easier to talk to than Dexter. The impossible task she had put up for herself was proving out to be quite possible but that didn't mean that Christian would suddenly want to help her just because he didn't know what to say. Then again, she couldn't help but feel proud – Eiko was never good at talking back to people and she avoided arguments as if they were the plague. At least that was what the younger Eiko used to do. Now? Well, she certainly felt more powerful than before. If life was a game, she most definitely would've leveled up right at that very moment.

"Christian," Eiko said.

He glanced up.

"Will you help me?"

Chapter 12

Dexter was sitting in his room, mindlessly staring at the wall. He felt extremely bad for yelling at Eiko and kept telling himself that he'd never do it again, though that didn't mean that he wasn't guilty. The boy knew she had only tried to help, except that she couldn't properly understand the situation. It wasn't her fault, in fact, it was his own – he should've been the one to explain it to her. Then again… it was far too late for that. Eiko had already left the dorm and was most likely feeling just as bad as he was, except for the fact that she wasn't guilty at all.

Dexter covered his face with a pillow and groaned. He wanted to scream although his tired body didn't grant his wish. Instead of spending the rest of the day being depressed in bed, though, he managed to gather the needed strength to get up and drag himself to the desk. He pulled the wooden chair, ignoring the way it loudly creaked against the matching floor and plopped on it. He put his forearms on the desk and stared through the small window – Dexter could see a few students passing by. There were the plastics who were going towards the girls' dorm and he couldn't help but wonder which one of them was Kate. Then there were a group of boys who seemed just like him. *Nerds*. He wondered whether he'd have found his place in their little anti-social group had he not met Eiko.

The boy's brows furrowed in frustration when the thought of her passed through his mind yet again. No matter how much he tried to free himself from the negative emotions, it seemed that Eiko followed him like a haunting spirit.

"Why do I even care so much?" He groggily asked himself as he looked away from the window. Less than a moment later, he grabbed his school bag, placed it on his lap and started searching for his notebooks. "It's not like we've been friends forever." When he found the needed book, he pulled it out of the bag and threw it onto the desk. A few more items followed and by the time he was done, the bag was light and almost completely empty. He placed it on the ground without a second thought.

"Damn it…" He mumbled out as he opened the first notebook. There were random scribbles on the first page, though the rest of the paper was neat, tidy and showed countless math equations. Dexter bit his bottom lip while looking up and down at the problems. Unfortunately, no matter how hard he tried to concentrate, he couldn't get anything right. Each attempt at solving an equation turned out to be pointless due to Eiko occupying his thoughts.

It didn't take long for him to let out a loud sigh of frustration as he pushed himself away from the desk and glared through the window again. This time there weren't any students except for one.

It was *Eiko*.

She had a wide smile on her face and Dexter felt a ting of anger run through his body. They had just been in a fight less than an hour ago and she was already smiling? He couldn't believe his eyes – there was no way Eiko didn't think of their friendship as important. The boy rubbed his eyes in order to make sure that what he was seeing was the truth. There Eiko was, happily walking along the campus towards the girls' dorm. *Wait a minute…* Dexter narrowed his gaze. Even if he was atrocious at math, he still knew enough to be able to find out the location of the girl's departure. Considering she was right beneath his window and was walking in the opposite direction of his dorm…

Dexter shook his head and went back to his bed where he fully laid down. He covered his face with his hands before running them through his hair. *Maybe she felt bad and came to personally apologize to me? But… She looks way too happy for someone who hasn't gone through with what they want. Then why was she in my dorm? Was she even here? Am I just hallucinating things because I feel guilty? No way…*

There was no use for him to keep on thinking about her and he couldn't help but curse the human mind for being so weak when it came to arguments. No matter what happened, he knew he had to confront her the following day in order to let everything out. It would be easy, at least in theory, but in real life he didn't know what he'd say or do. He still didn't even know what he was being so bothered for. He had gotten into plenty of fights with his old friends but most of them were guys. Girls were a whole other territory – they were scary and unpredictable. Eiko seemed cool, though, so he didn't think she'd hate him forever.

Still the thought of whoever had made her smile was lingering in the depths of mind.

Chapter 13

Eiko threw herself against the bed with a loud thud. She yelled out a loud 'yes!' and victoriously pumped her fist in the air. She couldn't believe that she had managed to convince Christian to help her! It was all so surreal as if it was a hidden level in a video game. She was finally starting to get used to the mechanics that St Ambrose carried with it, along with its wide variety of students. Eiko never would've thought that she'd be able to get on the good side of a bully but she realized that life had plenty of surprises.

In order not to let her excitement get the better of her, though, she grabbed her phone that was charging throughout the whole morning and spent the rest of the day catching up on her mobile games. As much as she wanted to bring justice to the school, she knew she had to take it slow and cautious in order to avoid stirring up trouble and getting expelled.

Wait… Wasn't that what Dexter had told her?

She paused her game and lowered her hands, the phone's screen now mere inches away from her face. Her features showed a thoughtful frown. Even if he was rude to her for no reason, she still hoped that he was doing alright. Eiko shook her head and unpaused her game.

She didn't know when she had fallen asleep but she was sure she hadn't gotten enough of it when the loud and annoying alarm woke her up. Her whole body jumped in surprise, eyes wide in shock as the cogs in her brain tried to help her figure out where she was and what exactly was going on. When she pushed herself with her arm, she realized that there was cold glass against it. Eiko quickly backed away and grabbed her phone, holding it close to her chest as she mourned the dead battery after trying to turn it on multiple times to no avail. It was obvious she forgot to close down each application she was using, which in turn ended up draining all her battery.

That wasn't so bad – it was not like she could use the device in school anyway.

Eiko stiffened at the thought of class starting without her. She mentally cursed at herself for spending so much time trying to turn on her phone. The girl's morning rituals were almost fully skipped. She knew she didn't have any time to lose. Even if the scar on her hands had healed, she still wasn't looking to create a new one. Eiko swiftly put on her uniform and grabbed her school bag without checking what was inside – she was aware that most of her important books were in her locker. The gamer didn't bother checking whether she had left her front door open and practically half-jogged down the stairs, her tired and confused mind making her forget about her previous falling down. By the time she was at the entrance of the school, there weren't any students around.

Eiko's stomach dropped in anxiety as she pushed the front door open and stepped into the main building. A quiet sigh of relief escaped her lips when she realized that the hallway itself still had a few students lingering here and there. Thankfully, she managed to get to class on time. Eiko took a deep breath before opening the door leading to the History room (it was a habit she had formed during her stay at St Ambrose) and quietly made her way inside. She sat on the front row due to still being the last student to enter the room but she didn't seem to mind it. After all, she saw Christian sitting in the corner.

They hadn't talked much after he agreed to help her, unfortunately. Even if his cold demeanor had cooled down a bit as the conversation went on, he told her that they were done talking and that she should leave lest she grab anyone's attention. The warning was cryptic, if anything, though Eiko listened to it nonetheless. That was the least she could do when it came to helping Christian out. She knew she still had a long way to go before fully earning his trust but she had a good start so far.

That was one problem out of the way. Now, Eiko had to tell Dexter that Christian was going to join them. She lightly grit her teeth, not realizing that she was pressing the pen far too hard against the sheet of paper. When she ripped it, she gasped in surprise. Despite the sound being quiet, it still managed to get the attention of all the students and the teacher due to the room being extremely quiet.

"Is there something you'd like to share with us, Eiko?" The teacher asked. Her lifeless stare destroyed what little confidence Eiko had.

The girl frantically shook her head. It took a few seconds for everyone to get back to copying from the blackboard. Eiko wanted to plop onto the desk and just hide her face forever – she couldn't control the blush of embarrassment that had spread across her features. When she accidentally glanced up at Christian, she saw that he was smiling at her. He looked… *weird.* He wasn't wearing the usual smug smirk she was always faced with. Eiko was quick to look away from him. They still had plenty of time to talk after class ended but right now she had to do her best to copy everything because she knew there weren't any tutors around. If she failed more than three exams, she'd be out. Not that it was a bad thing, of course, but now she felt like she was far too invested into finding out St Ambrose's dark past, plus she couldn't just leave Dexter alone even if she was mad at him.

The lesson passed relatively slowly. That was the case with most classes early in the morning – Eiko's brain kept begging her to let it sleep but she couldn't. When she closed her eyes for a few seconds and felt the relief of unconsciousness wash over her, the teacher's loud voice instantly woke her up. By the time class ended, she had almost fully forgotten about her scheduled meeting with Christian. It was weird that was she was doing with Dexter she was now doing with his *bully*. A part of her felt bad but... There was no way Christian would continue hurting Dexter any longer. They were all on the same side now and she wouldn't allow anyone to get hurt no matter what happened. That didn't change the fact that the bully looked completely disgusted at the mere mentioning of the cosplayer's name.

"Come on, Christian," Eiko groaned.

He shook his head. "No way, dude. You'll never see me hanging out with that loser."

"But we need to work together."

Christian grimaced. "You never told me that he'd have to tag along with us."

"Dexter is cool." Eiko was quick to defend her

friend. "He can be a little weird at times but for the most part he's alright."

"He's a leech, that's what he is," Christian stated.

The gamer found herself at a loss of how to react. She had never expected for Christian to have such negative feelings towards Dexter. She thought it was a case of a random bully getting a random target that happened to be her friend. There wasn't supposed to be any deep reason.

"Why do you dislike him so much?" Eiko furrowed her brows.

The bully was the one who now looked surprised. "I—I don't..." He glanced away. "He's just lame and I know that he's using you."

"Dexter was the one who helped me get back my cell phone after *you* took it away from me." She grit her teeth. "He's not a bad guy. I know that if we work together we'll be able to find out the truth."

"I don't want to find out anything if it's with *him*."

The statement was extremely cold and Eiko could practically feel the negative energy radiating off of Christian. This made her think long and hard for her next words – she had to choose the right ones in order to successfully persuade him. Nonetheless, she couldn't help but be frustrated from the whole situation. She was so close to getting the team together and yet… It seemed that she had much more work to do.

"I'll let you play on my phone if you help us," Eiko suddenly stated.

Christian looked surprised. "What?"

The girl nodded. "Yup. I'm going to give you access to as many as five different dungeon crawler games with character customization."

"Who said I care about some stupid video games?" Christian defensively replied.

Eiko's lips curled into a confident smirk. "I mean it's obvious that this school's main goal is to take the fun away from everything." She lowered her voice. "Mobile games are one of the best source of fun there is, you know? Don't you want to fight scary monsters to save the world?"

"Uh… I've never thought about it," he mumbled out.

The gamer's smirk turned into a full-out grin. "Great! I'll show you how to play after we find the school's secret."

"Wait, you can't just persuade me with a game—"

Unfortunately for the boy, the school bell rang. If they didn't hurry up then they'd be late for class and neither of them wanted to get punished. At least Eiko had managed to win the argument this time. Even if Christian himself wasn't a gamer, she was sure he'd enjoy what she had to offer. The thought of her playing one of her tabletop games with him and Dexter was what kept her lively and excited throughout the rest of the school day, though she knew she still had to confront Dexter. She absolutely hated getting into fights with her friends but sometimes it was inevitable. Then again, she was sure that Dexter would be the easier one to persuade to join the mission. His personality was tamer than that of Christian and Eiko was certain that he'd be able to understand where she was coming from.

It was *supposed* to be easier although no matter how much she searched for Dexter, she couldn't find him. She didn't want to ask for Christian's help when it came to that, which is why she kept going from room to room during the short breaks the students were given. Much to her surprise, though, there was no sign of the cosplayer at all – it was as if he had vanished into thin air. By the end of the day, Eiko was extremely worried. Even if Dexter didn't have the best marks out there, he never skipped school.

Skipping class in St Ambrose was never worth it, Eiko sadly thought, *but where could he be? Is he in his dorm? Why*?

Despite not wanting to pour even more salt into his wound, Eiko knew there wasn't any other way. She needed to talk to Dexter as soon as she could in order to fix everything. If it wasn't for him, she never would've been so invested in finding St Ambrose's secrets. This is why she believed that he should be the one to lead the mission – he had the needed street smarts and charm.

Eiko didn't bother looking for Christian. Instead, she made sure to escape the main building as fast as possible in order not to see him or the plastic bullies. Thankfully, they all seemed to be talking with each other in the hallway, which led to Eiko cautiously sneaking around and avoiding their attention. When she got outside, she took a deep breath in order to calm her rapid heartbeat and without worrying about what others might think, instantly made her way to the boys dorm.

Her suspicion of Dexter not feeling quite right turned out to be true because when she knocked on his door, there was no reply. When she tried to open it, she found out that it was locked. A sigh of frustration escaped her lips as she placed her ear against the door and listened for any sort of movement coming from the other side. *What is it with boys and never opening their doors on the first knock?* Eiko couldn't help but roll her eyes in annoyance.

"Dexter, it's me," she quietly said. Despite the low tone of her voice, her words still echoed throughout the staircase. "I... I don't want us to fight anymore."

There were suddenly footsteps that could be heard. Dexter was coming closer. Eiko quickly backed away from the door and tried to act cool, as if she wasn't just being extremely creepy. When the door creaked open, she smiled.

Dexter looked awful, which caused the friendly grin to disappear. He had bags underneath his eyes and seemed to be completely exhausted. If Eiko didn't know better, she would've thought that he was sick.

"How... How are you feeling?" Eiko mumbled out, brows furrowed in worry. It was a stupid question but she was at a loss of what to say.

A shrug was given in reply. "I'm *feeling*."

"Are you still mad at me?" She sighed, and looked at her feet in despair.

Dexter slightly perked up in confusion. "I was never mad at you," he stated.

Eiko hopefully glanced up. "What?" She asked in disbelief. "B—But you yelled at me."

"That's why I thought *you* were the one who was mad at me. I was the one who was wrong – I understand that you were just trying to help," Dexter quietly said.

Eiko's smile had made its way across her features once again. "Forget about that." She shook her head and stepped inside the hallway leading to his room. "I've got awesome news!"

Dexter couldn't help but raise a brow in suspicion as he moved away so that the girl could enter and calmly closed the door behind her. "What do you mean?" He definitely hadn't thought that they'd get back to being friends like that. Maybe Eiko truly cared about him and his feelings.

"Okay so," Eiko started speaking, "I went and talked to Christian. Wait—Don't give me that look!" She huffed.

"Yeah, yeah…" Dexter rolled his eyes and folded his arms across his chest. "What'd he say?"

The gamer ruffled the back of her hair and made sure her bow was set in place. "Well… After a bit of talking I managed to convince him to help us! I think…"

"You... *think*?" Dexter tilted his head to the side.

A nervous chuckle escaped the girl's lips. "Yeah, kinda. He was a bit uh... Reluctant to work with us but I know that deep down inside he feels the same way. We all have the same goal in mind."

"Did you ask him about the newspaper article?" The boy mumbled out.

Eiko's lips curled into a sheepish grin. "Yes and no."

"Eiko, you literally had one job. *One*." Dexter grimaced.

"I know, I know," she whined, "but he was being super defensive about it. I don't think he trusts us that much yet but it's good that he's willing to work with us. We'll get to the bottom of it eventually."

Dexter sighed, "If we're lucky."

"We don't need luck on our side for this, trust me." Eiko grinned. "Now, what do you say about holding our first meeting today, leader?"

The cosplayer choked on his spit. He started coughing and covered his mouth with his hand. It took him a few seconds to compose himself before he leaned towards Eiko, eyes wide with surprise. "Did you just call *me* leader?"

Eiko's victorious grin was hard to ignore. "Yup. You're the one who wanted to do this so you should be the one to take the lead."

"Christian is never going to accept that," Dexter murmured.

The gamer shrugged. "Maybe, maybe not. He's not as bad as he claims to be."

"Right…"

Chapter 14

Dexter turned out to be right. When the trio got together for the first time and Eiko told Christian about who was going to lead the mission, the bully almost punched him right then and there, though the girl was quick enough to get between them. She hated having to play the role of the peacemaker in the group although without one, the two boys would surely kill each other. This is why she did her best to end each argument before it even started. The first meeting was full of tension, the air around them was uncomfortable and Eiko was beginning to regret gathering their team of three. By the end of the month, though, they all seemed relatively comfortable with each other. Christian wasn't mindlessly bullying Dexter even if he made snide and smug remarks each time the other boy failed doing something. When the cosplayer replied with just as much annoyance, the bully simply laughed and told him that he was learning to become cool.

Despite not thinking that being mean was a synonym for being cool, Eiko was glad to have the two boys finally getting along. Unfortunately, their research was slowed down due to the fact that the girl was practically banned from the library because she couldn't control herself whenever she saw a computer and the two boys kept on arguing on which book to take. Now that she wasn't there to stop them from fighting, she ended up waiting for over an hour outside. She had leaned back against the wall with her hands crossed over her chest, mind trailing off to her daily quests on her phone. There were muffled voices coming from behind the door followed by a loud 'shush!' that sounded through each time they got a bit higher.

Thankfully, Eiko's boredom soon disappeared when she saw a familiar figure in the distance. Sister Anne was quietly passing through the school hallway, holding a basket full of clothes. Her eyes were slightly narrowed and she was no longer smiling. She looked *off*, to say the least, but it was nice to find out that she carried her never ending kindness when she saw Eiko. Even if she wasn't smiling, she was still extremely polite.

"Good morning, Sister Anne." Eiko bowed her head in greeting.

It looked like the caretaker wanted to smile but it seemed that it was physically impossible for her to do so. "Good morning, Eiko. How have you been?"

"I've been good. School is just… school." She giggled. "What about you? You seem a bit tired— I'm sorry if that's rude, I didn't meant it like that."

Sister Anne shook her head. "Don't worry, child. You're not rude, you're right. I have been feeling quite spread out these days. There's just so much work to do…"

It was weird to be called a child especially by someone like Sister Anne. Even if Eiko hadn't spent a lot of time with her, she knew that the woman considered her an equal which is why she had decided to help her in the first place. Now she was calling Eiko a kid – she sounded like she was becoming more and more like the rest of the staff. Sister Anne was one of the nicest and most pure people Eiko has ever met, which is why she felt a sudden inspiration rush through her. She would no longer be trying to find out the truth about St Ambrose due to curiosity; she would do it to save Sister Anne as well.

Before the girl could ask about the reason for her feeling so exhausted, the door leading to the library suddenly opened. Both Eiko and Sister Anne jumped in surprise and glanced at the two boys. Dexter was looking up and down an old thick newspaper, whereas Christian was holding two hardcover books. By the time Eiko looked at the caretaker, she was already gone. It was as if she had vanished into thin air, just like Dexter when he had locked himself in his room.

"Who was that?" Christian was the first one to speak.

Eiko shook her head. "It doesn't matter," she sighed. "Anyway, what did you two get?"

"This is supposed to be the origin of the article Christian found." Dexter held up the newspaper, pointing at the other boy with his free hand. "He got the first yearbook ever made here."

"*And* the most recent one," Christian added by clearing his throat.

Eiko grinned. "Good job guys." She clasped her hands together. "Now we need a private place where we won't be bothered."

The two boys looked at each other for a moment.

"My room, duh," Christian firmly said.

Dexter couldn't help but roll his eyes. "But we did it in my room last time."

"I bet your room smells like dirty socks." The bully backed away.

Eiko loudly coughed in order to get their attention. She then placed her hands on her waist and gave them the look of a disappointment mother. That certainly wasn't the time for them to start bickering.

"What about your room?" Dexter suddenly turned to her.

Christian nodded even if he was surprised at himself for actually being on the cosplayer's side for once. "Yeah, that'd make the most sense."

The gamer held up her hands in a defensive motion. There were more than a hundred reasons why she couldn't let them get near her room and most of them started with Kate. She couldn't begin to imagine the countless rumors and full-blown bullying the plastic girl and her groupies would subject Eiko to just because they'd see her with two guys. Not only that, but the fact that she disliked Christian would only make matters worse.

"How about *never*," Eiko firmly said.

The boys laughed at her and she felt a slight blush of embarrassment spread across her features. "Alright, alright." Dexter grinned. "How about we take turns? We could go to Christian's room now and the next time we get together we could go to mine. How does that sound?"

"That works, I guess." Christian shrugged.

Eiko nodded. "Yeah, that's perfect."

Even if the decision was spontaneous, none of them complained about it for the rest of the day. The walk to the boys' dorm was quiet, although the silence wasn't as awkward and tense as before.

Christian was leading the way with Dexter in the middle and Eiko cautiously glancing behind her in the back. When they made it to the bully's room, the girl made herself feel at home – she sat on the bed and stretched. Dexter, on the other hand, was acting shy and quiet. His gaze kept moving to the girl and then to the bully until Christian told him to sit wherever he wanted. They were supposed to be working together, right? Letting someone lame touch his stuff wouldn't be the loss of the century.

The rest of the afternoon was spent searching for any sort of clues. Dexter was the first one to finish inspecting the newspaper and, unfortunately, he didn't end up finding anything much to Christian's surprise. They almost got into an argument due to the bully claiming that was where he found the article. When he took the paper in his own hands, though, he realized that no pages were missing. It was brand new. Christian shook his head and threw the newspaper at the floor out of frustration. Both Eiko and Dexter jumped, and he had to apologize for startling them.

Eiko didn't manage to find anything interesting either. The portraits of the students from last year definitely looked creepy but that was most likely because of the old vintage style they were taken in, as if the school couldn't afford to get a proper cameraman who used a camera from the twenty-first century. They all looked like lifeless ghosts staring right through her soul and she couldn't spend more than a few seconds looking at each picture without feeling anxious. She kept thinking how that would be her fate as well if she didn't do anything to stop it. When Dexter came to her side in order to ask to go through the book, she gave it to him without a second thought and stood up from the bed.

Even if she was facing Dexter with her back, she could practically *feel* his distaste for the pictures. Trying not to dwell on the dead eyes of the previous students, Eiko made her way towards the desk where Christian was situated. When she asked how it was going, there was no reply. The boy stood completely still, staring at one of the pages as if he was hypnotized. Eiko bit the inner side of her cheek and leaned in to take a stealthy glance at what he was looking at.

There was a loud gasp that sounded throughout the room.

Chapter 15

"It's time for school, sweetie. You don't want to be late."

A soft feminine voice spoke out, each word pulling the sleeping boy to the brink of consciousness from his deep slumber. There was darkness at first – it soon faded into light as the boy opened his eyes and squinted from the bright rays of light attacking his vision. He groaned.

"Come on, Christian. You'll be late."

The boy sighed. It took him a few seconds to fully get up from the bed. His stomach was hurting and he felt completely exhausted. He definitely didn't want to start school but wasn't left with any other choice. What was once a cheerful and happy boy had turned into a quiet and reserved child. Christian was forced to leave all his friends behind after his parents moved. It wasn't anything surprising and each time he kept on clinging onto false hope that they'd stay in one place for at least once. Unfortunately, due to his father being part of the military, they had to move quite a lot. This made Christian very frustrated but he knew he couldn't do anything to persuade his parents to listen to him. He hated it when his father got mad and started yelling, and he hated his mother each time she got into one of her manic moods. The only friends Christian had were imaginary. As he got older and started middle school, though, even they left him to his own devices.

St Ambrose Middle School was supposed to be one of the best schools around and despite his parents wanting the best for him, that didn't change the fact that he was completely alone and lacked social experience at such a young age. The school itself looked frightening, if anything. There was a sense of dread that washed over the boy's body the moment he stepped through the wide iron gates. He wanted to back off at that point but he ended up bumping into his mother's stomach. She gently pushed him forwards and he saw that her lips were curled into a wide grin when he turned around. It was as if she was glad to be getting rid of him.

"Don't worry, dear. Mommy will come visit soon."

She never came.

The days went on but Christian's hope was not lost – at least not until the end of the school year. He kept on looking through the window of his dorm, waiting and waiting and *waiting*. Eventually he got old enough to understand that there was no point in hoping for something that wasn't going to happen. His parents had long left him and Christian couldn't help but feel extremely stupid and pathetic for wanting to see them again. He hated his parents but most of all, he hated himself.

Was I not good enough?

I never complained.

I never cried.

I tried to be the perfect child and yet... You still left me.

You left me when I was a kid.

How could you?

How dare you?!

The negligence created a new person, a new Christian. He would no longer be a scared child, he would fight for himself and for what he believed in. There were no more mental barriers that kept his impulse control down, no point in trying to be someone he wasn't just to please his ungrateful parents. His whole personality changed. Even if he was faking it at first, it didn't take him long to find his place in the role of a bully. Each scared glance given towards him from the other students made him feel powerful; he felt like he was in control for once. It was a risky situation – a risky addiction born from the fear of others. Christian knew he couldn't keep on doing whatever he wanted without the teachers noticing, though he had made a promise to himself to continue for as long as he could.

It turned out that the staff hadn't really cared about his endeavors. It was Kate who ratted him out to the Principal and got him in trouble the first time. He had bullied one of her groupies without knowing, and she wasted no time in contacting the higher-ups. He couldn't believe that someone like her would care about her friends – she seemed like the type of person to betray even herself if it meant becoming prettier or smarter. Then again, that was a battle Christian couldn't win. Kate was the perfect student if you didn't count her tendency to put on makeup and combine the school's uniform with flashy accessories. She also had a way with words and her charm had no end, which is why when she accused Christian of bullying her *and* her friends, he couldn't defend himself.

Christian couldn't remember much from the meeting with the Principal. It was like his mind was trying to protect himself from what happened. Even if he didn't know the exact way everything transpired, he still knew that Kate was to blame for his punishment – he was whipped ten times across the back and was forced to stay in school for over ten hours each day due to detention being extremely long. That was a month of his life he hated.

Unfortunately, his suffering didn't end there. His grades started dropping and Kate made sure to verbally abuse him each time she passed by. The worst part of it all was that he couldn't even tell anyone – no one would believe him either way. Christian had taken the role of the bad guy but he never expected it to be so agonizing. He felt more alone than before even if he had managed to make a few friends after joining the sports club. The boys that didn't fear him were those who respected him no matter what he did. They were mindless drones who would follow him to the end.

Christian hated people like that.

Everything changed when Eiko arrived, though. There was something about her that lured him in, something about her that was *different*. Even if he had never spoken to her before, he knew that he had developed a crush on her the moment he laid eyes on the girl. Unfortunately, due to not having enough experience talking to girls and having normal conversations with people, he tried to do the only thing he could – bullying. Even if he was surprised to see an actual cell phone when he first confronted Eiko, he knew he had to play it cool. He acted as if he wasn't impressed and instead of asking her about how she managed to bring such a device there, he was the one to take it away from her. In a way, he was trying to protect her because if someone from the school's staff managed to find out about it, then she'd get in serious trouble. The girl's look of hatred made his stomach drop and the presence of Dexter made things even worse. Why had Eiko chosen Dexter, of all people, to be friends with? He was lame and had bad marks.

Christian knew he was better.

As much as he liked Eiko for her looks and personality, though, that didn't change the fact that he got very mad upon realizing that she had been to his room. A part of him was embarrassed, although another part was frustrated. He was mostly angry at himself even if he wouldn't ever verbally admit it. He didn't want to play the role of the villain anymore because he knew that Eiko would only end up hating him. Unfortunately for him, though, that was the only role he knew how to play. When Eiko confronted him a second time, asking question after question about the stupid article Christian didn't even care about, he couldn't let his true feelings out. The boy just wanted to confess to her, get rejected and then move on with his life but he couldn't – not with Dexter there. Despite not knowing the cosplayer's true intention of hanging out with Eiko, he always assumed the worst. This is why Christian ended up deciding to actually help the girl with her idiotic attempt to find out what was going on St Ambrose.

Christian knew that she'd end up regretting ever getting involved.

Nothing good ever came out of St Ambrose. The first meeting with the Principal had left him completely shaken up. There was just *something* about that man that made him seem like he was out of this world, like he didn't belong there. His smiles never reached his eyes and he always wore the same clothes even as the weather changed and got hot or cold. Each time he set foot on campus, all students stopped talking to one another and could only stare in shock, eyes following each and every movement made by the Principal as if they were prey looking at a predator, praying that they wouldn't get killed. Kate was no exception – even if she was confident when lying to the man, Christian could still see her lower lip quiver as she spoke to him.

He didn't want Eiko to get into trouble. He didn't want her to get hurt but he'd make her even more suspicious of him if he told her to back off. It hadn't worked the first time; why would it work the second? The best thing he could do was to tag along and make sure she was safe, even if he hated Dexter's guts. Christian was trying to be a better person, he really was but it was proving to be difficult...

Especially after Eiko saw *his* picture in the

yearbook.

Chapter 16

"It's… It's you."

Eiko's shaky voice was the only thing that could be heard in the deathly silent room. Dexter glanced up in confusion. Christian could only emotionlessly stare at the picture.

"Really?" Dexter asked in disbelief. He stood up from the bed and made his way towards the two students on the desk. "Oh…"

"This is the first yearbook. It's… It's from over ten years ago," Eiko mumbled out. "How is that even possible? You're our age. I'm sure of it – we share the same classes. Christian, what's going on?"

The bully let out a quiet sigh. There was a headache starting to form around his temples the more he listened to Eiko. "Remember when I told you it's none of your business? Well, I meant it."

"What's that supposed to mean?" The girl couldn't hide the frustration in her voice. "What does *this* mean? We're supposed to be helping each other, right?"

Christian shrugged. "If Dexter would actually use his glasses instead of just wearing them like an accessory, he would've read that this is the first yearbook of students to be punished."

"Students to be... punished?" Eiko quietly asked.

Dexter huffed. "Who even are the rest of the students here? I've never seen them before."

"I don't know them either," Christian calmly replied.

"How do you expect us to believe you now?" The girl snapped. "How do we even know if anything you've told us so far is actually true?"

Dexter gently placed his hand on the gamer's shoulder in an attempt to calm her down. "Eiko," he mumbled out.

The girl instantly slapped his hand away. She was furious. "We've wasted almost two months searching for information. We went through each newspaper article, we read so many books. Was it all for nothing? I can't believe you!"

There was a loud slam against the desk. Christian had hit it with his fist. Both Eiko and Dexter stiffened, though the girl didn't back away. She was far too angry to be scared that she'd get hurt. When she quieted down in order to give room for the bully to defend himself, he ended up standing up from the desk. Eiko instantly grabbed him by the wrist but he roughly pushed her away and she ended up bumping into Dexter, almost making them both fall to the ground. Before she had time to stand up, the door leading to the staircase slammed shut.

Eiko and Dexter had found themselves alone in Christian's room.

"Are you alright?" Dexter was the first one to break the heavy silence.

Eiko instantly replied. "No, I'm not!"

"Sorry…" He trailed off.

The girl was leaning against the desk. She placed both her hands over the wood and grit her teeth. The corners of her eyes were burning with tears and no matter how much she tried to compose herself, afraid that she'd embarrass herself in front of her best friend, she couldn't stop the tears from falling down. Eiko quietly sobbed and took heavy breaths. Her heartbeat was strong against her ribcage and she felt worse than when being bullied by Kate. Soft hands formed fists as Eiko bit on her bottom lip in a vain attempt to stop her tears.

Dexter could only stand in the distance, not knowing what to do. He didn't want to make everything worse. His brows were furrowed in worry and he felt like crying, although it wasn't because Christian had lied to them – it was because Eiko was so devastated. In a way, Dexter felt responsible for everything that had happened. He was the one who edged Eiko to start looking for the mysterious article but he never would have thought that she would get so obsessed with it.

And now?

She was the one who got hurt.

"I—I can't believe he was lying to us the whole time…" Eiko shakily spoke through the loud sobs. "I tried so hard to get him on our side. I just… I just want us to be happy." She glanced through the window in front of the desk. There were groups of students heading towards the main building; it was dinner time. Eiko didn't feel hungry at all. "Is that so much to ask for?"

"We'll find a way, don't worry," Dexter mumbled out. He took a step closer although he didn't touch the girl without her permission. He didn't know how she'd react if he placed his hand on her shoulder again.

"No, we won't." Eiko shook her head. "It's… pointless. There's no use for us to try anymore."

"You don't mean that," he stated.

The girl wiped her tears away with her sleeve. She felt like she could finally breathe again even if her stomach was tied in knots. "Look what happened."

She sniffed. "Christian never meant to help us. He just wasted our time. Everyone here is evil."

"No, they're not," Dexter murmured. He finally decided to place his hand over the girl's shoulder in order to give her a supportive squeeze. "Christian isn't either. They're just… misguided. I'm sure we can save them."

"Please," Eiko sighed, "I just want to be alone right now. I don't want to talk about them."

Dexter was quick to take the cue. He left the room without any protest and made sure to head to his own home as fast as he could. Even his worry kept on increasing by the second, he still respected Eiko's wishes and could only hope that she could hang on and wouldn't do anything stupid. He didn't know how she had persuaded Christian to help them, nor did he *want* to know. Dexter knew from the beginning that the bully would be hard to work with and the only reason he didn't say anything about it was because Eiko's smile of happiness was the most important thing. Now he felt guilty for letting the whole situation happen. If he had spoken up about his suspicions then it most likely wouldn't have happened but, unfortunately, it was far too late for him.

Eiko's heartbeat was still as rapid as ever even if the anger flowing through her veins was starting to disperse. When the frustration faded away, she felt disappointment – *despair*. As much as she wanted to stay positive and find a way to fix things, she couldn't. Eiko always gave people the benefit of doubt, although Christian had abused her trust over and over again. *How could he lie to me straight in the eyes*? The girl ran a hand over her face and realized it was hot and wet from the tears. The mere fact made her want to start crying again but she didn't want to stay in Christian's room anymore. In fact, she didn't want to have to do anything with him. The bully was just like the staff members. His sole purpose was to prevent her and Dexter from having fun and, much to her dismay, he ended up succeeding.

The boys dorm was completely empty. There were no students passing by that would question her reddened face, except for Kate and her groupies who were getting ready for dinner time on the opposite side. Eiko could care less about them or what they'd say and do to her. She had no intention of avoiding them as if she was a scared vermin and just went straight towards the girls dorm. Of course, Kate's eagle eye instantly spotted her. When she called out her name, though, Eiko didn't respond and instead kept walking. It didn't take long for Kate to roughly grab her by the shoulder in order to spin her around so that she could look at her.

"What do you think you're doing by ignoring me, loser?" Kate's loud voice boomed through the whole campus.

Eiko's eyes were lifeless. She didn't even bother looking at Kate – she stared in the distance.

Kate's lips curled into a grimace as she shook the girl. "Hey! I'm talking to you!"

Much to her surprise, though, Eiko didn't react. She looked (and felt) like a zombie. The plastic girl was starting to get creeped out. She didn't know how to react. The once anxious and cowardly girl was now completely emotionless.

"Come on, Kate. Let's just go."

Eiko couldn't help but let out a loud sigh of relief as she continued on with her journey back to her room. By the time she unlocked her front door, she was crying again. The girl felt stupid for being so emotional, the stress from the sadistic teachers and Christian's betrayal were all too much for her. The only thing she could do was lie down on her bed and cry herself to sleep.

Everything was awful and she just wanted to go home even though she knew that was impossible. Eiko would be stuck in St Ambrose until the first vacation.

Chapter 17

As autumn passed by and winter took place in the forest surrounding St Ambrose, the whole campus became white and soft with snow. The weather was extremely cold but most students went back home to their relatives in order to spend Christmas with them. The whole area was devoid of any sort of life other than a few staff members. There was a rumor that even the Principal himself had gone back to his wife and child, though the origin of it was unknown. Nonetheless, the heavy and tense energy surrounding St Ambrose had faded away with the last days of autumn. Now, everything was calm and quiet. There were no birds to loudly chirp each morning, no crickets to echo into the night. The main road was blocked by snow. Not only was the weather extremely chilly, but it was almost always dark. The little source of sunlight could barely cover even half of the campus and because of that, the lamps around the main gate and dorms were left on most of the time. The feeling of despair was stronger than ever, especially because there were a few students who weren't so lucky.

Eiko was supposed to head back home a bit later due to her mother being busy with work. She had told the girl that she wanted to get some extra money so that she could get everyone in the family the presents they deserved. Unfortunately, with the heavy snowfall fell and the possibility of reaching St Ambrose with a car swiftly faded away.

Eiko was completely devastated at first. Even though her mother kept calling her over and over again in order to make sure she wasn't taking it too bad, at one point the girl stopped picking her phone up. She wasn't the best at hiding her emotions and she didn't want to make her parents more worried. She knew she had to be strong in order to make it through the vacation. Eiko couldn't afford to daydream about possible scenarios nor did she have time to feel sorry for herself. She wasn't the same person she was when she first started school. The gamer was much stronger now and could fight for herself.

Being stuck in St Ambrose had its perks, despite the fact that it was so depressing. There was no one to force the students to wear the ugly grey uniforms and even if different staff members kept giving her dirty looks, no one actually bothered to tell her to change. They had no authority over her during the vacation, which left Eiko with a vast sense of freedom when it came to exploring.

Alone.

The girl drifted away from both Dexter and Christian after the latter was exposed to be lying. After various attempts to confront her and talk about what had transpired, Eiko didn't give the bully any space to try and redeem himself. Christian wasn't worth her time anymore, he had already wasted enough of it. Even if Dexter was a whole different person and he was only trying to help, he always ended up making Eiko frustrated. He couldn't save the situation no matter how much he wanted to and ended up saying the wrong thing. After getting into multiple fights with him, Eiko swore off all contact with the cosplayer. She did it in order to protect both of them from each other.

That didn't mean she was going to give up on finding out the school's dark and dirty secrets, though. In fact, that was the only thing keeping her stable even during her darkest days. Whenever she lost hope and wanted to give up, she remembered the strange piece of newspaper article that was the source of all negativity in her life. If she and Dexter hadn't seen it, then things would be fine – they would still be friends and would be happy. It was as if she was cursed, though. The mere thought almost made her laugh. You see, Eiko had created a new character that she used as a main in most of the online games she played on her phone – she was a warrior class now and all melee classes were usually extremely weak against curses and hexes. She couldn't help but feel as if she truly was becoming the physically strong although mentally weak Barbarian. Each time she looked at herself in the mirror, though, she could only shake her head with a sheepish smile. Eiko was tiny and thin. If anything, she would be one of the casters whose purpose was to make the melee players' lives a living hell.

Despite not knowing what class she'd be in real life, Eiko had managed to define a role for each teacher. Unfortunately for her sanity, most of them had stayed behind during the winter vacation. They definitely didn't look like women with families and it certainly wasn't because they were dressing up as nuns. Their personality wasn't the best – it was as if the Principal had chosen the most unstable women on purpose. Nonetheless, they still fell into a specific norm of people.

Sister Anne continued to be Eiko's favorite, despite becoming a bit more distant as time went on. She was the person the girl spent the majority of her day now that they were both free. They bonded over their young age and Eiko even let her play some of her mobile games. She felt that it was only right – after all, she never would've been able to get her phone back had it not been for Sister Anne's help.

Sister Anne was a healer. A Cleric.

Then there was the Math teacher – Sister Helen Marie. Like most people in that specific sphere, she was extremely stuck up, rude and sadistic. When she wrote on the blackboard, she made sure to do it as quickly as possible before moving on with the next equation. God forbid there was someone who wanted to ask a question, especially if she had explained the topic mere minutes ago. She started yelling, screaming as if she was being attacked by a demonic foe. The students learned quick enough not to ask anything or to speak in general.

Sister Helen Marie was a damage dealer. She fit the role of a Warlock.

When it came to the History lessons, things weren't so bad. Sister Mary Bernadette was the total opposite of Sister Helen Marie. She was very small and quiet, and she didn't care whether people paid attention in her class. She wasn't too keen on punishing troublemakers and they all respected her for treating them like people... Except for when she wasn't in the mood – that was when she became the Devil himself. If Eiko could describe the way she acted during her random mood drops, she'd compare her to Sister Helen Marie, although *worse*.

Sister Mary Bernadette was also a damage dealer but she wasn't as scary (most of the time). She would definitely be a Sorceress.

Science class was... *interesting,* to say the least. Sister Mary Mercy didn't fit the name given to her;

she showed no mercy when it came to failure. Despite not spending any time on explaining the chemical equations she made them learn by heart and not by understanding how they work, she had the audacity to be mad at the students when they failed the many surprise tests. Even if she didn't raise her voice, she still kept on threatening them with the Principal.

Sister Mary Mercy was yet another damage dealer. Her colorful experiments reminded Eiko of a talented Wizard.

Shop class was weird. It certainly was unique compared to the rest of the classes, though Eiko didn't know whether it was in a good or bad way. Sister Ursula was the quietest teacher she had ever come across. It seemed like she didn't care about teaching at all and wanted to head back home more than all of the students combined. She was extremely lazy and spoke very slowly, though most of her words were slurred and impossible to understand. Each time a student asked for help, she just rolled her eyes in reply and continued on with her magazine.

Sister Ursula was a Rogue. Eiko had a hard time choosing a definite class for her but after spending a few hours deep in thought, she figured that a Rogue was most suitable for her. Even if she was lazy, she could be quite deadly. It was almost as if she was stealthily hiding behind the persona of an uninterested nun. She wasn't trustworthy, that much Eiko knew.

Physical Education was supposed to be fun. Despite never being too big on sports, Eiko still enjoyed watching her classmates play volleyball. Of course, St Ambrose had done its best to keep the fun away from most of the students' favorite class. Sister Carla acted like a dictator. She was always carrying a wooden cane in one hand, which she slapped them with whenever they ran in the school gym. The first time Eiko saw someone being punished for running during PE, of all classes, she couldn't believe her eyes. Unfortunately, after the punishments kept becoming more and more severe with each unwritten rule broken, most students lifelessly stood around when they were supposed to be playing with each other.

Sister Carla was a Warrior, no questions asked. She wielded her cane like a mighty two-handed weapon that was able to kill all monsters in a single blow. If she were in an online game, she'd definitely be one of the most overpowered people.

Last, but certainly not on a scale of evilness, was Father Fitzgerald. He taught Theology and even if he had an omnipresent passion for the subject, he was one of the most terrifying figures Eiko had ever come across. She couldn't possibly imagine the Principal himself being scarier than Father Fitzgerald. The teacher had an everlasting grimace spread across his features and it was impossible to please him no matter what she did. The best students in Eiko's class had all fallen victim to despair after receiving a "you should do better" on their works, despite having the maximum score. It was as if Father Fitzgerald was living in another plane of existence where score and numbers had a whole different meaning. Eiko could still remember the first time she had Theology class even if she tried to forget it no matter what. That specific subject had become one of her biggest fears and each time she had to go back to the cursed room, she felt extremely anxious. The rest of the students felt the same – they all gave each other frightened glances as they waited for the teacher to show up. Yes, despite being a perfectionist on another level, Father Fitzgerald was almost *always* late for class. As much as the students wanted to get a few more minutes of sleep, none of them had the courage to go against Fate and be late themselves for once. They all suspected the man of trying to test them.

Father Fitzgerald didn't fit any of the class stereotypes Eiko was familiar with. He was a whole different human being and no matter how much she thought about it, she couldn't come up with something specific that fit his behavior. The man was a strong mix between a Rogue, a Warrior and a Warlock.

Nonetheless, all of the school staff was extremely difficult to deal with. They were all impossible to please and they longed to find out that someone had messed up. Eiko became desensitized to their behavior and could focus on her work without being too bothered. Kate's bullying also mellowed out over the months and now that the plastic girl was gone for such a long time, the gamer couldn't help but relish in the mental and physical freedom she had been given. That didn't make her mission any easier, though. In fact, it was now much harder than before because she didn't have Dexter and Christian's help but she knew she had the power inside her to see things through the end. If there was someone out there who could find out what was going on behind the scenes in St Ambrose, then it most certainly was Eiko.

One of the main problems she had was going to the library. Eiko was aware that there were countless books and documents left to be deciphered, especially yearbooks containing the names and pictures of students who were going to be punished. That had raised a red flag in the girl's mind and she couldn't stop thinking no matter how much she tried to distract herself. In order to get to the rest of the yearbooks, she had to get past the librarian who disliked her. Eiko regretted ever letting her emotions get the better of her after seeing the computers in the corner, although there wasn't much she could do about it at that very moment other than to try and sweet-talk her way into being let in.

As she had expected, the librarian wasn't happy to see her.

Eiko awkwardly slithered inside the vast library and she prayed to the RNG gods that the woman there would continue being engrossed in the daily newspaper she was reading. Unfortunately for the girl, the moment she stepped inside, the wooden floor loudly creaked and alerted the librarian who ominously glared at her without even knowing who she was at first. Eiko couldn't help but let out a sigh of despair before she defensively raised her hands and backed away from the main desk. The librarian didn't say anything, she simply pointed at the front door.

The gamer lightly shook her head as she took a deep breath. "Would it be possible if I—I could start using the library again?" She shakily asked. "I promise I won't be loud. See? I can whisper."

The librarian rolled her eyes. "If you make even a

sound, you'll get kicked out. Understood?"

"Y—Yes ma'am." Eiko gulped.

It didn't take the gamer long to quietly move away and get to the interior of the library. She cringed after each taken step as the floor creaked loudly but it seemed that the woman on the desk was aware of the sound, which is why she didn't immediately kick Eiko out. Even if the girl's stomach flipped in excitement when she saw the old computers in the corner, she managed to contain her emotions and did her best to act like they weren't there at all. The girl still had her phone, which is why she didn't actually miss her own laptop that much, though it definitely would've been nice if she could use it again. Eiko didn't realize her features had twisted into sadness but thankfully there wasn't anyone around who could mock her for it. The gamer started going through each cupboard in her search of the school's yearbooks. She regretted not asking Christian where he got them but she believed it wouldn't be that hard – there were only so many books she could go through. For a moment Eiko thought about asking the librarian but she quickly realized she didn't want to bring any more attention towards herself and what she was trying to do. The last thing she wanted was for a staff member to find out her true intentions. This is why she silently continued her quest.

Minutes turned into hours and Eiko's legs were burning from standing up so much. For a moment she thought the librarian was going to kick her out, though her worries turned out to be in vain. The woman went for an afternoon coffee break, leaving Eiko completely alone in the library. The girl didn't even know whether the librarian was aware that she was still there – she suspected that the old bat had forgotten about her existence. There was silence that suddenly filled the whole room as bright eyes cautiously glanced to the computers in the other part of the library. Eiko quickly looked at the door and then back at the devices. It didn't take her long to make up her mind and, after taking a deep breath in order to calm her burning nerves, she stealthily made her way towards the computers. They weren't anything amazing, at least on the outside. The gamer gently sat on the wooden chair in front of the device on the left and booted it up. Much to her surprise, nothing seemed to happen at first even if the whirring sounds of the computer's fan were obviously there – the screen itself stood black for over a minute before suddenly lightning up. It showed St Ambrose's logo but there was no password. It seemed that the computers were only to be used by staff members because there were no fancy wallpapers nor were there different folders of projects and drawings. This made Eiko even more suspicious of the school. Even if she knew that St

Ambrose was extremely old-fashioned, it still didn't make sense that such devices would be forbidden. It wasn't like there were any games that could be downloaded – there was no internet connection. Eiko leaned down and inspected the back of the computer box in search for a cable that could be used to connect her to the internet. Unfortunately for the girl, though, there wasn't anything like that. What was weird was that there were three different icons of the school's logo. None of them had a name and they could only be told apart by their color. The icon on the left was red, the one in the middle was yellow and the one on the right was blue.

Eiko felt a cold shiver run down her spine. It looked just like a trap set for curious students like her. Had the librarian planned all of that? Was she the one who installed the suspicious-looking programs? Could they possibly lead to the same thing?

Oh man, Eiko sadly thought, *I don't really know if this is worth it.*

She suddenly perked up. *The Principal isn't here*, she smiled, *so I can't get in trouble even if I get caught, right? Then again... The librarian lady is already scary enough. Ugh, what should I do?!*

The monitor suddenly went black.

Eiko's stomach dropped in anxiety and she swiftly glanced behind her. There wasn't anyone there; the librarian was still out for her break. Before the gamer had time to react, the screen turned back on. Two of the icons had changed their colors – the yellow icon was now green and the blue one was purple. The red logo was the only one that stood untouched. Eiko couldn't help but raise a brow in suspicion as she finally put her hand on the mouse and double-clicked on the crimson icon. A window popped up, taking up most of the screen. It shifted a few colors before leading Eiko to what seemed to be a front page. It definitely wasn't a site, though, that much was obvious. It turned out to be some kind of registration form with a lot of personal details. The weirdest part was that it was impossible to change the current date.

There were the usual details of Name, Last Name, Age, Occupation – stuff that didn't really interest Eiko. As she scrolled down, though, her jaw dropped in surprise. There was an empty field of 'Names of students in class' and 'Number of students made miserable'. Eiko had to blink a few times in order to make sure that what she was seeing was right.

Is this supposed to be some kind of report? She clicked on the 'Name' field. Suddenly, all the teacher's names showed up. She realized she could scroll through them and change the basic information based on the name and class. The program was using an auto-fill function except for the last field about the students. Before Eiko had the time to go through and each and every name, though, she heard heavy footsteps in the distance. The girl loudly gasped in surprise as she leaned downwards in order to turn the computer off. No matter how much she tried, nothing happened. The screen was still showing the running program and there was no way for Eiko to turn it off.

The girl quickly stood up from the chair and started frantically looking around, doing her best to ignore the anxiety born from the now much louder footsteps. She went to the widest cupboard facing the corner wall and cautiously leaned against it as she slowly sunk to the ground. The door leading to the library creaked open and Eiko held her breath in order to prevent herself from making any kind of noise. The heavy footsteps continued until they suddenly stopped after a few moments and the girl figured that the librarian had reached her desk. The small feeling of victory soon faded away when she heard the woman's deep and raspy voice.

"Huh? Where is that brat?"

Eiko bit the inside of her cheek, reaching for her chest with one hand in a vain attempt to calm her rapid heartbeat. She almost burst out of the room the moment the familiar footsteps could be heard, although for better or for worse she stood completely still as if she wasn't there at all. The librarian started looking around the whole room. She kept getting closer and closer to Eiko; the girl could practically feel the vibrations across the floor from the heavy steps but before she was discovered, the woman set her eyes on the blinking screen in the distance.

"What the?!"

The footsteps suddenly backed away. They were much quicker than before and Eiko let out the breath she had been holding throughout the entire time. She slowly dragged herself up from the floor, staring at the librarian's back as she made her way towards the active computer. There was no way for Eiko to play innocent in order to avoid getting punished – the reason she got banned from the library was because she was excited to see the computers. Of course the woman would instantly know it was her and not anyone else, which is why Eiko decided that she didn't want to stick around and would much rather lock herself in her room and not come out until the winter vacation ended. She didn't want to risk getting seen by, well, *anyone* at that point.

The gamer used the distraction made by the computer to exit the library for good. She left the front door open, not wanting to make any sound and half-jogged through the corridor, all the way to the main entrance. Thankfully she didn't pass any of the teachers she knew in the hallway, though she still felt sick to her stomach. This was the first time Eiko had gone against the rules of the school on her own. Dexter and Christian weren't around to help her – she was all alone. The worst part was that they couldn't share the punishment when she did end up getting caught. Eiko's whole body was shaking as she cautiously made her way back to the girls dorm. The staircase seemed longer than ever and by the time she was at the top of the building, she passed out.

Chapter 18

The days passed by slowly. Despite Christmas being right around the corner, Dexter felt *empty*. The excitement born from the mere thought of receiving presents and gifts was no longer present. Each time his younger siblings tried to talk to him about it, he ended up snapping at them. The boy felt bad for not being able to control his emotions, though he was far too stressed yet unable to share his problems with his family. They didn't understand – he had tried talking to them before to no avail. They kept saying that he was only dramatizing his stay at St Ambrose and that the school itself wasn't so bad, in fact it was one of the more elite middle schools around. There was no way for him to prove the awfulness of it all due to not having a phone, which is why he gave up. That didn't mean that he didn't get frustrated each time someone asked him about St Ambrose.

His mother stated that he was simply going through puberty, which is why he was always frustrated and felt like no one understood him. Perhaps that was the case, though Dexter always prided himself on having control over his emotions. Each time he snapped at a family member, however, he realized that he wasn't in control as he previously thought. This was one of the main reasons why he distanced himself.

As Christmas came and passed by, Dexter felt even worse than before. His thoughts kept trailing off to Eiko and what she could be experiencing all alone at St Ambrose at that very moment. The girl having to stay in the school was no secret – if Dexter's parents had been late by even just a day, he would be in the same situation as her. The snowfall took everyone by surprise and no matter how much he wanted to go back to the school in order to help the girl, he knew it wouldn't be possible. Despite his sense of righteousness being omnipresent, the cosplayer couldn't ignore the fact that Eiko had treated him awfully the past few months. She had become extremely distant and stopped sharing any information. Simple questions, such as "How are you?" turned into arguments and it didn't take long for Dexter to realize that they would be better off alone. That didn't mean he liked it, though. In fact, he'd be lying if he said he didn't miss her and the adventures they had together.

Much to his frustration, though, people changed.

He knew that Eiko was going through emotional turmoil after Christian's betrayal and he also felt hurt, but he'd never think of abandoning her in the middle of their mission. Dexter didn't even know whether she was continuing with it at all and, frankly, at that point he didn't even care. There was one thing that was for certain: St Ambrose wanted to suck out all the fun students could possibly have. It had managed to do it to Eiko and Dexter as well, even if they were the only one who were actively fighting against it.

"Hey, Dex!"

A childish voice pulled the boy out of his thoughts. He slightly jumped and glanced to the source of the voice, finding out that it was his younger sister Melanie. She was five years old and often expressed her desire to start studying in St Ambrose whenever she got older. The cosplayer wanted to gag each time she started talking about his demonic school.

"What's up, Mel?" He ly asked, standing up from his bed. When he realized he couldn't hear her that well, he remembered that he was wearing headphones that were plugged to his computer. After gently removing them, he made his way towards the doorframe where his sister was standing.

"It's time!" She widely grinned and her voice shook with the excitement she felt. "It's time!" She loudly repeated.

Dexter couldn't help but tilt his head to the side in confusion. "Time for what exactly?"

"Oh my gosh, Dex! It's the day after Christmas.

Let's open presents! Let's do it!" Melanie was quick to scold him.

The cosplayer let out a sigh. He really wasn't looking forward to spending even more time with his siblings, who for sure hated him for being such a Debbie Downer. Nonetheless, he didn't have much of a choice. Dexter let himself be dragged down the staircase by Melanie and by the time they got to the living room, his two brothers had already opened their presents. Jack, the older one, was cautiously holding a big plane prop like it was made out of glass and was about to break at any moment, even if the material was most likely expensive and stable cardboard. Ian, the younger brother, was holding a big box of a figurine. When Dexter stepped closer, he saw that it was one of the main characters of a show they all used to love to watch together. In a way, the cosplayer felt nostalgic about the past, though he knew that he couldn't turn back time no matter how hard he tried. The best thing he could do was to get used to the present.

"Dex, look!" Melanie's voice loudly sounded throughout the room again. "It's so pretty!"

The boy hadn't event realized that his sister wasn't holding him by the wrist anymore. When he glanced at the tall and colorful Christmas tree, he saw Melanie sitting underneath it, holding a plush bear. It was almost bigger than her and had a pink bow around its neck. The girl was tightly hugging it.

"Yeah, it's nice," Dexter calmly commented.

"What did you get?" Jack suddenly asked.

All the attention was now placed on the cosplayer and he couldn't help but feel awkward. He let out a nervous chuckle, lips curling into a sheepish smile. "Uh... I don't know yet. Wait, I'll check right now."

"Seriously?" Ian laughed. "We've all been waiting for this day, dude. Haven't *you*?"

Dexter waved his hand around. "Yeah, kinda. Sorry, I've just got a lot of things on my mind. Anyway... Let's see what we have here." He knelt down next to Melanie and started going through the multiple colored presents in search of the one that had his name written on it.

"Duh, that's obvious. You've been acting like a total as—" Jack was interrupted by Ian's hand around his mouth.

"Dude, language! Not in front of Melanie. If she tells mom, we're all going to get in trouble," he scolded his brother.

Melanie perked up at the mention of her name. "Mom?"

The two boys defensively raised their hands and, in order to take the attention away from what Jack wanted to say, they started asking her questions about the plush bear she still had her arms wrapped around. Melanie was happy to oblige. Even if the was the youngest sibling, she was the one who talked the most.

Dexter rolled his eyes in annoyance. Despite being the oldest brother, he didn't want to deal with his younger siblings' problems. He still knew that he was the most mature out of them all, though that didn't change the fact that he was an introverted loner. The cosplayer used the distraction created by his brothers to continue looking for his presents. It didn't take him long to quickly skim through the front row only to find nothing. After each box placed on the side, he felt the familiar yet uncomfortable feeling of despair set in his gut. Right when he was about to give up and go back to his room, acting like he wasn't bothered at all, he managed to see his name written on a small blue box with a red bow wrapped around it. The boy carefully pulled it from beneath the tree and lightly shook it against his ear in order to get a clue as of what could possibly be inside.

Instead of opening it right next to his siblings, Dexter was quick in his decision to slither back almost completely unnoticed into his room. He didn't want to answer any questions, nor did he want to get made fun of if his present didn't turn out to be anything special like the others. This is why he made sure to lock his door before sitting on the bed, placing the small box on his thighs. He took a deep breath before untying the bow. It was easy enough, for better or for worse, and he found himself staring at tiny container. It really wasn't that small, although when compared to the boxes of his siblings' presents, it certainly wasn't anywhere close to being their size.

Much to Dexter's surprise, though, his present turned out to be exactly what he needed.

It was a cell phone – it was small and thin, though it looked brand new. There was a charger, along with earphones in another small box and he almost yelled in happiness. He couldn't believe that his parents were actually letting him have such a device. Not only that, but he would now be able to help Eiko when it came down to gathering information and clues.

Dexter's wide smile suddenly disappeared. His chest hurt from the negative emotions going through his body, born from the thought of losing the girl forever. Even after all that time, he still blamed himself for dragging her along the impossible mission. It was his fault she got obsessed with finding out the truth and getting hurt by Christian's manipulation. No matter how much he wanted to apologize, he knew he wouldn't be able to do it – at least not until school started back up again.

"If only there was a way for me to find out her number…" Dexter mumbled out, laying back down onto the bed. He stared at the ceiling deep in thought.

The boy didn't know whether minutes or hours had passed when the idea sprung into his head. He quickly jumped off the bed and ignored the way his vision blacked for a moment. Without wasting any precious time, he went back downstairs in search for his mother. When he passed through the living room, he saw that none of his siblings were there. The only things that could be seen were the few empty present boxes and candy wrappers thrown about the floor. Dexter couldn't help but shake his head at their lack of etiquette, though he didn't care enough about them not getting in trouble to clean up their mess. Instead, he swiftly made his way to the kitchen in search of his parent. Much to his despair, though, the room was just as empty as the last one. He glanced around just in case, realizing that there was a yellow sticky note placed on the door of the fridge. The boy pushed his glasses back with his index finger as he took a step closer. A loud sigh of frustration could be heard when he read what was written on the paper.

'We're going New Year's shopping.   Take the dog out for a walk and   don't   cause   any trouble! Your dad   will be back late at night.

Love, Mom'

Dexter leaned against the fridge, placing his forehead against the cold door. He couldn't believe his awful luck! If there was anyone who could help him get in touch with Eiko, it was his mother. She was the one who dealt with everything St Ambrose related and he was sure she had done her research on all his classmates. Despite her cheerful behavior, she was extremely paranoid and was afraid of anyone in the family getting hurt. This is why she had the tendency to be overprotective and spend days upon weeks, looking for information about everyone *and* everything. Dexter certainly got his hunger for knowledge from her, even if his grades were horrible.

The only thing he could do was wait.

Chapter 19

There was heavy darkness all around. Distant voices came and went, saying things that were impossible to understand. Eiko's whole body felt heavy and no matter how hard she tried to open her eyelids, she couldn't. It was as if they were glued shut. When she tried to move her body, she realized that the case was the same. It wasn't until one of the distant voices became much closer that she finally felt like she could get a firm grasp on consciousness. Her eyes grudgingly opened and she pushed into a sitting position on the soft bed. It didn't take Eiko long to find out that she was in the nurse's office once again, except that this time Dexter and Christian weren't there to help her. Instead of them, though, was someone Eiko had hoped to never see again.

The librarian was standing in front of the girl with her hands crossed across her chest. She was glaring at Eiko – there was no mercy in her gaze despite knowing that the girl had most likely passed out on her way back to her room. Eiko suddenly felt sick again. She laid back down and turned her head to the opposite side, acting like she didn't know what was going on. When she heard her name get called out, though, she let out a tired sigh of frustration.

"Eiko, someone is here to see you." The nurse's

voice was calm and uninterested. She was still sitting at her desk next to the door frame and most likely didn't know what had transpired. This made matters even worse because she couldn't defend Eiko.

The girl prayed that Sister Anne would magically show up to save her, however life was far from a fairytale. The gamer had to be her own savior in order to continue with her mission. That was the least of her worries at that very moment, though. Her flight or fight response had activated and she wanted to jump out the window just so she could avoid having the much dreaded conversation that would only end up with her getting in even more trouble. Much to her dismay, she wasn't given any other choice than to lie down and listen.

"You little rascal!" The librarian loudly croaked. "How *dare* you even get close to the computers?! Did you not promise that you'd behave? You do know that lying to a St Ambrose staff member is an incredible offense."

Eiko glanced at her with tired eyes. "I—I didn't know…" She mumbled out, realizing that her throat was extremely dry. "It wasn't my fault, I just… I just…" The gamer became silent for a moment as the cogs in her mind twisted and turned, searching for a lie that would be easy to believe. "The computer turned on by itself so I just... Went to check if everything was alright. I didn't even click on anything."

"Lying is unacceptable!" The woman yelled. "You have gone through documents that are forbidden to students. Once the Principal arrives, he will be told of your misadventures."

The gamer instantly tensed at the mention of the man running the whole school. "Documents?" She asked in disbelief. "I haven't—I haven't seen anything like that! There was just a page of a site and... That's it. I didn't touch anything, I just took a look at it for a moment. I don't even remember what was written on the page."

The librarian shook her head. "Just you wait. You'll get the punishment you deserve."

And with that ominous statement, she exited the nurse's office. Eiko furrowed her brows in worry and glanced up at the ceiling, biting her bottom lip. She was already beginning to regret her actions; she knew she shouldn't have touched the computers but... They were right *there*. If only they were, well, normal, then she would've been able to turn them off and continued on with her day as if nothing had happened. Of course, nothing was actually normal in St Ambrose and she was beginning to realize that more and more as the days went on.

The only good thing about the whole situation was that the Principal most likely wouldn't be back until the end of the vacation which still had a full month left. This left Eiko enough time to think about her next course of action. She needed to come up with a more believable story in front of the headmaster. Even if a part of her actually wanted to get expelled so that she could continue her life in a new school, she knew that she was far too deep to back out now. For better or for worse, the curiosity had gotten complete control over her. Eiko knew much more than before, except that she didn't exactly know what to do with the information. There wasn't anyone to share it with and it was strong enough evidence to get the school in trouble. She still couldn't be sure whether the site wasn't a fabrication created to hide the truth, though judging by how defensive the librarian got, there had to be some truth behind it. The woman surely must have seen the site. Why would she refer to it as a document, though?

The more Eiko thought about the incident, the more frustrated she got, thanks to her inability to form a conclusion. Instead of feeding her ever-growing headache, the girl focused on getting the needed rest she lacked. She hadn't even realized she was skipping sleep being far too busy trying to decipher old books and newspapers. Not only that, but she also looked up countless of articles on the internet regarding St Ambrose and its 'wonderful' staff members. There wasn't anything negative to be found on the internet and the reviews left by the older students were all five stars. It was extremely suspicious.

By the time Eiko made her way back to her room, again, this time without passing out so close to victory, she opened her door and instantly laid down on her own bed. Yes, the stairs had turned out to be a pain to climb up, though she managed to do it. In order to reward herself, she decided to play one of the game on her cell phone. As she booted it up, however, all interest in gaming suddenly faded away. Even after trying to do her daily quests, she still couldn't bring herself to play for longer than a few minutes at a time. This was completely shocking to her – she didn't know what was going on! Video games were supposed to be her main source of entertainment, especially during school although the strong feeling of apathy had surprisingly taken over. Eiko wanted to throw her phone against the wall in frustration but managed to control her anger. Instead of wasting anymore time trying to force herself to do things she didn't want to, she decided to focus on going through the internet in search of more information about St

Ambrose. Reading different articles was much more fun than doing stuff that was usually considered a hobby. The tides had turned in an awful way, leaving Eiko confused as of why she didn't enjoy the things she had before. Was she finally letting go of her past persona, evolving into a new person that would become another robotic student of the school? She shook her head. That wasn't possible because she still wanted to let the world know about how awful St Ambrose was.

There was suddenly a completely new article on the front page of the search engine. It read: 'St Ambrose Middle School – good or bad? We have interviewed the Principal and asked him some popular questions that will help you choose the correct school for your children.'

Eiko couldn't help but tilt her head to the side in confusion as she double-tapped the screen in order to gain access to the site. There were a few seconds wasted in loading, though when the main page showed up, Eiko was forced to squint due to the sudden contrast of colors. The whole page was littered with neon pinks, greens and yellows, making an instant headache form the more you looked at it. The title of the site kept changing colors every so often, making it hard to pay attention to the article itself. Thankfully, the interview was placed on a white page with a black font. That didn't change the fact that the site itself looked like a student's colorful IT project. There was no professionalism used in its design and Eiko found herself doubting the legitimacy of the whole domain. Nonetheless, she still went through the interview because she wanted to learn more about the Principal.

Is that why he's not here? Why would he be doing interviews now, of all times? Shouldn't he be back home spending Christmas with his family?

There were quite a few questions going through Eiko's mind even if none of them had a definite answer, except for the last one. She knew she wasn't the person to be judging him for not spending time with his family because she was in the exact same boat as him. Of course, she wanted more than anything to get back home to her parents and be littered with countless of presents from them, her siblings and grandparents. Unfortunately, sometimes bad things happened to good people. The best thing Eiko could do was to live with it and use her newfound free time to continue on with her investigation.

Which is what she did.

The gamer spent the next half-hour reading the interview. It definitely wasn't anything interesting – it had the same questions she had seen countless times before and the Principal, despite being described as smiling, was very cryptic in his answers. Most questions were answered with statements such as: "If you come to St Ambrose, you will find out."

Eiko couldn't imagine any parent going through the conversation and thinking that St Ambrose was a decent school, though apparently the publicity it had seemed to work well enough considering how many students there actually were. The only weird part about the article was that the Principal avoided certain questions regarding the past of the school with cut-out answers and questions of his own. Of course, there was the fact that there was no picture to be found of him anywhere across the page – or the whole internet, for that matter. It was as if the Principal was some sort of entity hiding his face in order to conceal his intentions. That would mean that real life would be like a video game, though, and Eiko was sure that wasn't the case. Perhaps the man was very old and didn't want others to make fun of his looks. Then again… She didn't think that anyone would risk their lives doing something as childish as that. Each time the man was brought up in a conversation, everyone around seemed to freeze in their movements as if someone had pressed a 'pause' button. That included the staff members, too. She had yet to see the way Father Fitzgerald would react upon the mention of the Principal, though she had for certain seen a few of the Sisters, including Sister Anne.

It seemed like there was an unspoken rule about the Principal and even if no one seemed to know why they feared him so much, they couldn't change their mind no matter how much Eiko tried to calm them down. She had decided to do a social experiment after reading the interview – she went around the school in search of the other few unlucky students like her who were stuck in St Ambrose during the most wonderful time of the year, and asked them what they knew about the headmaster. All of them had the same look of fear in their eyes.

No matter how much Eiko wanted to find out more information about the man running everything, it didn't take her long enough to realize that asking something like that from the other students was a waste of time. This is why she decided to meet up with Sister Anne the next day. Thankfully, neither of them were busy with work and chores, even if the older woman still had to keep everything under control. Sister Anne was a bit thinner and paler than before, though she still carried her friendly smile that made her easily approachable wherever she went. Eiko saw her outside – she was sitting on a bench leading to the side of the campus that consisted of a grass field. When the gamer got closer, she realized that Sister Anne was feeding the pigeons by throwing tiny crumbs of bread. Eiko couldn't help but smile, despite approaching her from behind and knowing that she wouldn't be able to see her friendly expression.

"Good morning, Sister Anne," Eiko politely said as she sat on the small wooden bench. It slightly creaked from the new weight.

The woman was startled at first, though she soon resumed her feeding. "Good morning, Eiko. How are you?"

"It's kind of cold," she sheepishly smiled, wrapping her hands around her arms in an attempt to show her distaste for the chilly weather, "but I guess I'm not bad."

"Please make sure to take good care of yourself. I was told you had a trip to the nurse's office yesterday..." Sister Anne trailed off. "I hope everything is alright."

Eiko felt her stomach drop. The memories of the previous day flooded her mind, leaving her with no escape when it came to dealing with the agony that flowed through her veins. She instantly removed her hands from herself and let them freely rest on her side as she glanced into the distance. Most of the pigeons were already gone, though there were still a few who were lingering and waiting for another piece of bread. They were much smaller and thinner than the ones who had taken all the food before, and Eiko couldn't help but find beauty in the way natural selection worked.

"It's not really but…" The girl sighed. "This is my life now. I'm stuck here, in St Ambrose." She motioned to the side with her hand. "And I'll get punished as soon as the vacation ends."

"Punished?" Sister Anne raised her voice even if her tone was still as soft and gentle as ever. "What happened?"

Eiko glanced to the side, biting her inner cheek in order to keep herself from venting and telling everything to the caretaker. Even if she did trust her with her life, she couldn't allow herself to make the woman an accomplice – that way they'd both get punished. "It's a long story," she replied.

Sister Anne had now scooted closer to the girl. She placed the bag of bread crumbs on the right side of the bench and kept her gaze locked with Eiko's. The woman's brows were furrowed in worry as she spoke, "Is there any way I can help?"

The gamer's shoulders slightly slouched and she found herself looking up at Sister Anne from the corner of her eye. Eiko made herself seem as innocent as possible – she was acting as if she was a hurt doe looking for its savior and in a sense, she actually was. "Well…" She took a deep breath. "I've been trying to find out more information about the Principal here. I've never seen or spoken to him so I was just curious." Eiko kept her voice in a quiet whisper.

Sister Anne looked conflicted. She opened her mouth to speak, although no words came out at first and she ended up slightly backing away. The woman was no longer facing Eiko – now, she was mindlessly staring off into the distance. "Is that why you got in trouble?"

A nervous giggle escaped the girl's lips. "Nope. I'm sure you're surprised but this isn't the reason."

There was heavy silence that followed. The darkness that surrounded St Ambrose was more noticeable than ever. It made Eiko feel even more anxious than before. It wasn't like Sister Anne to keep silent for so long; she either helped with whatever she was asked for or she politely declined. A strong gust of wind managed to make the woman snap out of her trance. She instantly looked at the girl again. "Ah, I'm sorry… I must have spaced out," she finally replied, "I'm not sure what I could say about him anyway."

Eiko was completely confused by that point. Was

Sister Anne actually trying to help her or was she simply feigning cooperation in order not to make the gamer sad. "Well, uh... What's he like, for starters?"

"He is different," Sister Anne whispered.

"Different?" Eiko dumbly repeated. "In what way is he different?"

The woman glanced at the ground in shame. "I have not met such a man as him before. He is... cruel." She clasped her hands together after placing them in her lap.

"He seemed pretty nice in the interview I read." Eiko shrugged.

Sister Anne's eyes widened in surprise and she instantly looked back at the gamer. "What interview?"

"I'm not sure when it's from but it got posted online yesterday," she said. "It's definitely from this year. The site is kind of weird, though."

The expression of disbelief was clear across the caretaker's young yet dried out features. "But... He is currently supposed to be with his family. I do not understand." She glanced away.

Eiko sighed. "It's fine if you don't believe me but,

here, I've got proof." She went through the left pocket of her thick winter jacket and pulled out her cell phone. Despite wanting to keep it a secret, Eiko still liked to carry it with her during the vacation mostly because there weren't a lot of students and teachers freely walking around. The article took a few seconds to load, though the moment it did, Eiko held up the screen on the level of the woman's face.

It didn't seem like Sister Anne wanted to read what was written on the page because the instantly gave a nod and squinted her eyes from the bright flashing lights of the site. "I see," she mumbled out, "well, he is the Principal. I believe he knows what is best for St Ambrose."

"Apparently not for his family," Eiko was quick to add.

Before Sister Anne had time to process the rude statement made by the gamer, Eiko's phone suddenly started vibrating. Both females stiffened in surprise and quickly glanced at the screen. There was an unknown number calling Eiko and she felt extremely awkward because it was happening right in front of the other woman. You see, Eiko never picked up when it came to unknown numbers – she didn't want to deal with any advertisements or scammers. She had her parents' numbers saved, alongside a few of her friends'. Other than that?

Nothing. And she liked it that way.

Much to her annoyance, though, she couldn't just turn her phone off just to be able to avoid extra human confrontation. She still wanted to keep the persona of a *relatively* good student. In fact, she was the perfect student if people were willing to overlook her powerful ability to always get in trouble no matter how impossible it could be.

"I'll leave you be." Sister Anne gave her a formal smile.

Eiko put her phone to the side and defensively raised her hands. "Ah, no—It's fine, it really is."

Before she even knew it, though, the caretaker was gone out of her sight. It looked like she had taken the bag of bread crumbs along with her and now Eiko couldn't help but feel judged by the pigeons who stared at her as if they were hypnotized, waiting for her to feed them. "Shoo!" The gamer motioned with her hand. "I don't have anything." She tried to raise her voice in order to scare them, however she was the one who ended up getting frightened from another strong vibration coming from her phone. It almost shook the whole bench.

I know that Sister Anne is gone so I don't have to pick it up but... Ah, whatever. Here goes. Eiko was quick to solve the mental argument. In a way, she longed for another adventure. Even if the caller turned out to be a random scammer, she could at least have a conversation with someone who wasn't Sister Anne or herself, and for that reason the girl finally picked up. She placed the device next to her ear and waited for any sort of sound.

There was random shuffling on the other side of the line and right when she was about to end the call, she heard a male voice. "Hello?"

Eiko froze. The caller's voice was slightly shake as if he was nervous to be calling her. It was impossible for him to be a scammer, nor could he be a random advertisers. After all, what those two had in common was confidence and the boy had none of it.

"Hi," she said. The simple reply did not make it any easier on the nervous caller. That was Eiko's true intention.

"Uhm... Who am I speaking to?" The stranger asked.

Eiko couldn't help but roll her eyes in annoyance. "You were the one who called me," she sighed.

"Yeah, yeah. I guess I was, huh?" He chuckled. "I just want to make sure I'm speaking to Eiko."

The girl's eyes widened in shock upon hearing her

name. She tightened her grips around the phone without even realizing. "Who is this?" She swiftly asked, voice firm and defensive.

"Eiko? It's really you, right? I'm so glad! It's Dexter, remember?"

The gamer found herself at a complete of how to react. She stood silent for a moment until her friend's voice snapped her back to reality.

"Are you losing signal? I can't hear you if you're speaking," he worriedly stated.

Eiko let out a breathless chuckle. She couldn't believe that it was Dexter, of all people, who was currently trying to contact her. She thought he'd never get near her again since her cold behavior towards him and even if she wanted to act distant because she was afraid of getting hurt once more, she missed her best friend far too much to be petty. "Dexter, oh my god," she murmured, "since when did you get a phone? How did you even find my number?"

"It was a Christmas present," he said. There was silence that followed until he awkwardly cleared his throat, realizing that Eiko couldn't get anything because she was still stuck in St Ambrose, trapped behind the never ending snow. "Mom helped me with your number. She tends to write things down like that."

Eiko shook her head. "I don't know whether to be flattered or worried."

"Don't worry, she's harmless." Dexter chuckled. "Anyway, I'm just calling to make sure you're alright."

Now it was Eiko's turn to awkwardly clear her throat. "Oh, uhm… Yeah. I'm fine. Everything is perfectly fine."

"You don't sound that convincing," he mumbled back. "What happened?"

"It's a loooooong story, Dexter. You missed out on some action." Eiko grinned, staring at the last remaining pigeon. It was pecking through the snow, trying to reach grass. She didn't even know whether pigeons were supposed to be outside during the winter but she couldn't just shoo it back to its home. "I'll tell you everything when you come here."

There was a sigh on the other end of the line. "I really want to be there for you, Eiko. You have no idea how bad I feel for you right now."

Eiko felt a twinge in her stomach. She suddenly felt like crying – each time someone expressed their sentiments, she always got emotional. "It's fine, I told you. I'm alive somehow but I still had to go to the nurse's office again."

"What?!"

The strong emotions coursing through the girl's body suddenly faded away and were replaced by the need to laugh. She breathlessly chuckled. "We've got a lot of catching up to do when you come back here."

"Yeah…" He trailed off. "Just make sure you survive."

Eiko couldn't help but raise a brow in suspicion. "Duh, of course I'll survive. My worst enemy is the snow right now. When the weather becomes warmer, I'll show it who's boss!"

Dexter grinned even if he knew she couldn't see him.

"Ah, never change, Eiko."

Chapter 20

"You have broken St Ambrose's rules time and time again. You have put the reputation of the school at risk. This cannot continue."

A firm, manly voice sounded through the quiet room. It shook the whole building with each word being spoken out. The room itself was basked in warm orange afternoon light as the sun slowly got hidden behind the hills and tall trees. One of the windows was open – the middle one – letting in cold winter air that made the whole situation even more dreadful. It was not refreshing, it was painful. There were three figures in the room.

"Your name was written in the book of punishment for a *reason*. You were given far too many chances to redeem yourself and yet you threw them all away. For what? What was so important to you that you'd risk your life?"

A cold gust of wind made the heavy black curtains move to the side, exposing the calm and bright background of the crooked trees covered in snow, matching the perfectly shaped white clouds. The sun was now completely gone, though it had yet to become dark outside. The sky had a light pink hue that faded into gray.

"I tried to help you, I really did but you did not let

me. You ignored each act of kindness and acted out of your own will, putting yourself and other students of St Ambrose in danger. That is unacceptable."

The man speaking started pacing around with his hands behind his back. The frustration and anger were evident across his features as he nervously paced around and bit his bottom lip, ignoring the way half of his body was lit up from the light coming from outside, whereas the other was basked in the shadow covering the entirety of the room. When he stopped, he turned to the student sitting on one of the two chairs in front of the big oak desk. His eyes narrowed down and lips pursed into a frown.

"You will be punished for your actions."

"But sir--" A feminine voice interrupted the man. "Isn't this too harsh?"

"Nothing is too harsh when it comes to protecting the school's honor. You have all given up your lives the moment you've stepped through the gates. Now, if you'll excuse me, I've got much better things to occupy my time with. Sister Anne, escort him."

She sighed but obeyed the command nonetheless. "Come on, Christian." The woman gently placed her hand over his shoulder as he stood up from the chair. "Let's get going."

It was safe to assume that Christian was severely distraught. His whole body was shaking out of both anger and fear, and his eyes stung with tears that were begging to be let out. He tried to be strong because he didn't want to make a fool out of himself in front of Sister Anne, however everything that had happened was far too much. He knew this day would come sooner or later, he just hadn't expected it to be so early. He wasn't prepared to deal with the consequences – Christian wanted to be a normal student just like everyone else. No matter how hard he tried, though, there was always something or *someone* that wanted to make everything worse. The boy could no longer control the vast amount of emotions coursing through his body. Before he knew it, there was tears trailing down his cheeks as he started loudly sobbing.

Sister Anne noticed his change of behavior and wrapped one of her arms around his back. She gently ran her hand up and down his arm in a soothing motion. "It'll be alright," she shakily whispered. It was obvious she didn't believe in her own words – her tone lacked confidence.

"I don't want to die," Christian mumbled out. He was shaking even more before – there were waves of hot and cold shivers running down his spine.

"You won't." Sister Anne hugged him closer. "I promise you won't."

Even if Christian didn't believe her, he still leaned into her touch. It was warm and soothing – she reminded him of his mother. Upon remembering his parents, however, Christian felt much worse than before. He had acted awful the last time he saw them: he was moody, frustrated and rude. Was that how they were going to remember him? If only they hadn't abandoned him then things would be different.

"Christian, please. You need to calm down." The woman quietly spoke as if she was talking to a stray animal she was trying not to scare. She didn't want the rest of the students to be curious about what was going on while she escorted him back to the boys dorm. They weren't supposed to know – that was the worst part of it all. St Ambrose had managed to get out unscathed after many scandals regarding the awful treatment of each students. Most claims were manipulated to be simple rumors.

"I can't calm down!" He loudly exclaimed, voice breaking off into a much higher tone. When he realized he was yelling, he glanced to the ground in shame. "He's going to kill me, I know he is."

Sister Anne let out a shaky sigh. She didn't want to lie to be boy, however she couldn't allow herself to make him even more distressed. It was obvious he needed therapy – he had the potential to be a good student and she had seen his multiple attempts to be perfect. Unfortunately, sometimes hard work turned out to be in vain.

"I know what the punishment yearbook is for," Christian added. "There's a reason I haven't seen any of those students. It's because they're *dead*."

Sister Anne quietly hushed him. She was never given permission to disclose information regarding what was going on in the shadow of St Ambrose. Due to her being quite new as an employee, she didn't know too much which is why she kept silent all the way over to the dorm. When they got to the entrance, Sister Anne finally let go of the boy and took a step backwards, clasping her hands together.

"Take care of yourself, Christian," she said.

The student wiped his red eyes with the sleeve of his shirt and sniffed. "Tell me." He took a deep breath. "Tell me what happened to those students."

Sister Anne's brows furrowed in worry. Her lips were pursed in an omnipresent smile and she couldn't stop herself from glancing down at the ground. "I can't, I'm sorry." She lightly shook her head. "Please... Try not to think about it too much."

"So you're just like the rest of them, huh?" Christian growled. The tears had faded away, replaced by anger and the awful feeling of betrayal. "You just act all nice so you can feel better about yourself. You don't care about anyone else!"

The caretaker quietly gasped. She couldn't believe that Christian was now attacking her, despite her trying to change things and make them better. And yet... He was right. Sister Anne was a coward. She couldn't stand up for herself and what she believed in because she was afraid of being punished. She could only stand aside and watch as countless of lives were ruined. Starting work at St Ambrose was the biggest mistake she had ever done, though she was now stuck there forever with no chance of getting out – other than death.

"You don't have anything to say for yourself?" Christian manically laughed. "I knew it!"

There was a crowd of students forming around, tempted to see what was going on. The boy's voice could be heard throughout the entire campus and Sister Anne felt worse than ever. She knew that backing away would result in her being shunned but she was left with no other choice. She simply couldn't argue with a student – she tried to help Christian, she really did, but it wasn't enough. He was too far gone. Instead of giving him the pleasure of responding to his taunts, she fully backed away and half-jogged to the main building. Her feet sunk in the snow which made it difficult to run and her socks became wet, though that was the least of her worries. When she went through the gates, she shut them and leaned against the cold doors. Sister Anne hadn't even realized that there were tears streaming down her face. She sunk to the floor and wrapped her arms around her legs, placing her head over her knees as she quietly sobbed.

She never wanted this.

She only wanted to make things right and yet no matter what she tried, it always ended up being in vain.

Chapter 21

Eiko was lying on her bed, staring up at the ceiling. Her right hand was tired from holding the phone for over two hours but she was having too much fun talking to Dexter, which is why she ignored the slight pain combined with needles prickling alongside the length of her elbow and forearm. A full month had passed after the Christmas vacation and most students were already present in the dorms. Dexter was currently being driven by his parents to St Ambrose but due to the roads still being littered with snow, the journey was turning out to be much longer. This is why the boy decided to call Eiko – to fight the inevitable boredom that came from each long car ride – and they ended up talking for over two hours.

Their friendship was weird. When they were apart from one another they constantly texted and called each other, and yet when they were together in school, Eiko had acted distant. That was, of course, because of the trust issues she developed from Christian's lies. She still kept calming Dexter down by saying that she the good old Eiko was back again, promising that she wouldn't ignore his existence. Even if Dexter was a bit worried, she was still his best friend and he believed everything she said.

The best part was that they were both still hyped about finding out St Ambrose's secrets. Eiko was stealthily continuing her research alone, though she was now being more cautious than ever after the second library incident. She didn't look forward to the meeting with the Principal, though a part of her assumed that the librarian must have forgotten about it because no one told her anything about there being such a thing. The Principal was back in school for over two weeks now and he didn't seem to be particularly interested in Eiko's misadventures. This was good because it let her focus on other parts of her research, such as going through the different buildings in search of clues and any hidden entrances. Even if Dexter laughed at her when she told him about her plan, telling her that life wasn't a video game and there wouldn't be any secret locations with bonus loot, he still wanted her to wait for him before continuing since he didn't want to lose out on any of the action.

Eiko acknowledged his request and stayed put until he reached St Ambrose. The pair had to cut the conversation short due to the boy's cell phone battery dying but, thankfully, the girl had plenty of things to do while waiting. Daily quests, dungeon runs, login bonuses – she could spend hours upon hours going through everything.

That didn't mean she wasn't excited when she heard

the faint engine of a car getting closer by the moment. She stood up so fast from the bed she felt blood rush to her legs and her vision blackened for a few seconds. Eiko leaned against the wall in order to maintain her balance until the darkness faded away and swiftly made her way down the stairs as fast as she could. Of course, she was still careful because she didn't want a *third* trip to the nurse, despite people saying that the third one was the charm.

By the time she got to the iron school gate, she realized that she forgot to put on a jacket and was freezing to death. Nonetheless, she still grinned through gritted teeth when she saw Dexter wave at her from the distance. It didn't take him long to head over to her and give her a hug while being careful not to drop the small suitcase he was carrying with him. He soon realized that she was shaking.

"Let me guess… You forgot to put on decent clothes?" Dexter sarcastically asked.

"What makes you think that?" Eiko feigned innocence, though there was smugness hidden in her tone. "Did the t-shirt gave it away?"

They both laughed with each other. It was nice seeing her friend again but Eiko still felt guilty for not treating him right. She just wanted to get her apology out of the way before they continued on with their day.

"Hey, Dexter. I'm really sorry about acting all weird…" She mumbled out as they both started towards the boys dorm.

Dexter's features twisted in confusion and he shook his head in reply. "You already apologized, Eiko, no worries. I just felt bad for not knowing what to do when you were depressed."

"I guess…" She sighed. "I'm just glad we're back to being friends again."

"Yeah!" He happily exclaimed. "You still need to tell me everything you've found out while I was gone."

Eiko's lips curled into a wide smile. Even if a lot of things had happened to her while Dexter was gone, she still managed to somehow escape relatively unscathed. Without thinking of what others were going to say about the two of them heading to the dorm together, she started explaining as many details as she could about the creepy librarian, the nurse and the interview with the Principal during Christmas. Dexter intently listened, taking in each tiny bit of information and keeping it locked inside his head in case they needed it once again. When Eiko was done, she let out a sigh of exhaustion as her shoulders slouched.

"Everyone and everything is creepy in St Ambrose. That's pretty much the short side of it."

Dexter breathlessly chuckled. "I kind of knew about that part already."

There was suddenly a loud bang that echoed throughout the walls of the staircase. The two of them stiffened in surprise and looked at each other with eyes wide in both confusion and paranoia. They stood completely still for a few seconds as if facing a blind predator, hoping that the threatening noise wouldn't be heard again. Unfortunately for them, though, just as they started walking upwards, it sounded yet again. This time it was even loud and they realized that they were inevitably getting closer to the source.

"Should we just ignore it?" Dexter whispered, taking slow and cautious steps.

Eiko hummed. "What if it's something serious?"

The cosplayer let out a small sigh. No matter what happened, Eiko still stayed the same kind person as always. She wanted to help everyone despite them not having any positive feelings towards her. Dexter didn't know how he felt about that – he admired her for being so brave and nice when faced with awful bullying and punishment from the teachers, though he also thought that she exposed herself far too much and would only end up getting hurt again. This is the main reason why he didn't reply and instead continued walking along the staircase, doing his best to ignore the loud bangs that made his stomach drop in anxiety.

When a yell could be heard, however, they realized that they were right next to the door where the noise was coming from. It was much louder than before and they realized that items were getting smashed and thrown around.

Eiko glanced up in horror, only to see that they were standing right next to Christian's room. She instantly looked back at Dexter with features twisted in worry. Her lips were pursed in a small worried pout and she didn't say anything due to not wanting to accidentally be heard by the boy on the other side of the door. She tugged Dexter to the side so that they wouldn't stand so close to it and leaned towards him so that he could hear her better when she spoke.

"We should—We should check it out," she whispered.

Dexter had a look of disbelief. "What do you mean? You still want to help him after everything he's done to you?" He slightly raised his voice.

Eiko instantly covered his mouth with her hand and glanced behind her for a moment just to make sure there wasn't anyone standing there, listening to them. When she turned back to him, her gaze carried sadness. "I just feel like it's the right thing to do…"

"Sometimes you need to let things play out the way they're supposed to without trying to change them, Eiko," Dexter quietly replied.

The girl's shoulders slouched in defeat. "But it's obvious something is going on. Are we seriously going to fight about this again?"

Dexter let out a sigh of frustration. "Fine. Just hide behind me in case something happens." He murmured, taking a step in front of Eiko and making his way closer to the door. That was until he felt a hand on his shoulder. When he turned to look at the girl, she shook her head.

"No," she said. "Let me do this."

"He might hurt you, Eiko. I won't let that happen," Dexter stated.

Eiko gave him a slight smile. "As much as I want a knight in shining armor, I can still take care of myself. I don't think he'll want to see you. Just stay close to me and be ready to act if something happens, alright? I trust you'll have my back."

"Yeah, yeah…" Dexter trailed off and moved out of the way so that Eiko could slither towards the door.

She flinched when another bang could be heard but after staying completely still for a few moments and taking in a deep breath in order to gather the courage she needed, she wrapped her fingers around the knob and pushed the door open. The narrow hallway was empty and the floor creaked with each step she took. She looked back for a second and gave a nod to Dexter who looked extremely worried. Despite the hallway being a short walk, Eiko still had enough time to think about everything that had happened between them and Christian. She still believed that he could be a good person and even if he played with her feelings and abused her trust, she wanted to find out the true reason for him doing that. It was apparent that he got very paranoid and anxious each time they started talking about the Principal and anything connected with him. It was weird seeing Christian, of all people, being scared. Then again, most St Ambrose students knew when to back down and flee in order to save their skin. Eiko wanted to break the toxic cycle, she longed to make people care about one another again.

The girl didn't expect to see Christian sitting on the floor, crying. The picture tugged at her heart and she felt herself at a complete loss of what to do. The boy's room was a total mess – the covers of the beds were thrown towards the wall and the chair and desk were almost fully flipped over. The only thing that was in its rightful place was the curtain covering the window, preventing what little light there was from coming in. The whole room was bathed in darkness and the only thing that could be heard at that very moment was the quiet sobbing of the boy.

"Christian?" Eiko quietly asked. She kept a safe distance between them no matter how much she wanted to run up to him and hug him.

The bully suddenly stiffened. He sniffed and tried to wipe the tears from his eyes with his sleeve before turning back in horror. He quickly stood up and backed away as far as he could. "Wh—What are you doing here? You shouldn't be here!" The boy raised his voice.

Eiko defensively raised her hands, taking a slow step towards him. She tried to be as cautious as she could, feeling like she was approaching a wild animal that was going to attack at any moment. "What's going on?" She gently asked. "I want to help you."

"No, you don't. No one does," he swiftly replied. His face was red from crying and his eyes were bloodshot. He had dark bags underneath his sunken eyes that showed his lack of sleep. The boy had also lost weight and now looked lanky and tall. This wasn't the Christian Eiko was used to seeing. He looked old and haggard. He looked and acted... *wrong*.

"I'm not mad anymore, alright?" She took another step forwards. "I can't help you if I don't know what's going on."

"You can't help me even if you wanted to and I know you don't. Stop pretending to be nice!" He suddenly yelled out.

Eiko froze in her steps, eyes widening in both fear and surprise. "What?" She shakily mumbled out. "But I... I want to help you."

"Please, Eiko. Please, please, *please* just leave me alone." He started sobbing again and tilted his head to the side so that she wouldn't be able to see his tears.

The girl couldn't move anymore. She found herself confused and hurt, but most importantly, she felt bad for the boy. Whatever had happened had obviously stressed him out. "We're friends, aren't we?" She softly spoke.

The boy glanced up. When their eyes met, she could

almost feel his pain.

"Sometimes friends make mistakes and that's fine. Trust me, I've messed up a lot before and I keep messing up now. What's important is to learn from your mistakes so you can become a better person." Eiko smiled. "You're already much better than when we first met. You changed in a good way – you stopped bullying and even if you lied to us, I know you did it to protect us from whatever is going on behind the scenes. Let us protect you this one time, Christian."

The boy let out a shaky breath as he slowly made his way to the bed and sat on it, holding his head with his hands. "I told you already. You can't help me even if you try. There's… There's no point."

"I can't help you if I don't know what's going on," Eiko repeated, "but I'll be here for you even if you don't want to tell me."

Christian stood there, completely unmoving. It was tough seeing him act so defeated – it wasn't like him at all. Eiko didn't want to accidentally make him feel even worse, which is why she still kept a safe distance between them just in case. When he didn't reply, though, she decided to speak again. "Did you get in trouble during the vacation?"

A sigh of frustration could be heard escaping his

lips. His fingers dug inside his scalp. "I'm *not* going to talk about it," he hissed, "just give it up already."

"How can I just act like nothing happened?" Eiko slightly raised her voice, doing her best to fight off the anger that was starting to bubble in her gut. "We worked together for almost half a year. I can't just act like I don't care about you."

Christian suddenly stood up from the bed. He held his gaze connected with Eiko's and screamed in frustration. His hands formed fists and his whole body was shaking. "It's too late," he said. "Don't make me regret my choice."

"Choice?" Eiko backed away. She couldn't fight against Christian's strong yet withered body as he practically pushed her out of the room. She almost bumped into Dexter on her way out. "What choice, Christian?"

Instead of a reply, however, the front door slammed shut in the girl's face. She leaned against it and ran her hands through her hair before looking at Dexter. He was giving her a look that said 'I told you so' and the girl thought she was about to get scolded by him.

"That certainly could've gone better," he sighed.

Eiko lightly shook her head in a vain attempt to get

rid of the negative thoughts. She pushed herself away from the door and followed Dexter as he started walking towards his own room that was situated on the top floor. "I don't know why he didn't want to say anything," she mumbled out mostly to herself.

"Well, you did kind of act like he didn't exist." Dexter teased her, despite knowing that now wasn't the best time to do anything of the sort. Nonetheless, he still wanted to lighten up the situation.

"Ugh, don't even start with that." Eiko rolled her eyes. "I acted the same way with you and we're still friends."

"People are different, Eiko." The cosplayer stated in a matter-of-fact voice. "Some of them want to deal with their problems on their own. I'm not saying that's a good thing but if it's what they want to do then... We can't do anything to help them. It's up to Christian to decide to open up. Until he does that... He can't be helped."

Eiko let out a small sigh. "That doesn't mean I feel any good about leaving him alone."

Less than a minute later, they both reached the boy's room. Dexter slowly opened the door and let the girl inside. Thankfully, the loud banging had stopped now that Christian knew they were both there but Eiko's worries did not ease even a tiny bit. In fact, the more she thought about him, the more worried she got. Dexter noticed her trembling but did his best to take her mind off what had happened.

"How are you feeling?" He gently asked before kneeling in front of his desk. He opened the first locker in order to go through the multiple files scattered across. They were all mixed which is why he had a hard time finding the different articles he had 'borrowed' from the library while him and Eiko weren't on speaking terms.

Eiko plopped onto the bed. "I don't know…" She mumbled out. "I just can't help but be worried for him."

"You've got a crush or something?" Dexter turned to look at her for a moment and stuck his tongue out.

The girl's cheeks flushed at the mere thought of her having a crush on anyone, and she defensively folded her arms across her chest. "No way. That's gross. I'm just worried about him the same way I was worried about you too."

"You're such a worrywart." The boy exclaimed. "We're all going to be fine, alright?"

"Yeah…" Eiko trailed off, showing her disbelief. "I hope so."

"I know so."

Chapter 22

Hushed whispers graced the campus of St Ambrose. The school field was littered with crowds of curious students. Nothing shocking ever happened at St Ambrose – daily life there was usually the same as ever. It was boring, full of chores and homework. This is why when a certain boy's portrait was placed in front of the main gate leading to the interior of the building, the students just needed to see what it was all about. Since it was a school day, Eiko and Dexter didn't find out about it until much later on after school ended. The crowd of students was omnipresent and they still cautiously glanced around as if they were afraid they would be caught looking.

Eiko discovered that something was terribly wrong when she saw a distressed Kate in the distance. She was surrounded by her friends who were trying to calm her down, although she ended up snapping at them. The plastic girl was usually very nice and kind when it came to her clique due to her being afraid she would lose her little army of mindless drones. This time, however, it didn't seem like she cared about making the wrong impression in front of the friends who idolized her so much. She had her arms wrapped around herself as if she was shielding herself from an invisible foe and kept nervously pacing around.

When Eiko and Dexter got close enough to hear what she was saying, the only thing they heard was the same phrase being repeated over and over again. "It's not my fault, it's not my fault, it's not my fault." Kate kept whispering to herself, not caring whether anyone heard her or not.

Eiko and Dexter gave each other a skeptical look. When they finally reached the crowd, the gamer realized she wasn't tall enough to see what was taking everyone's attention. She couldn't just pass through the students either – she knew she'd only end up getting pushed back. Dexter, however, was tall enough. The best thing she could do at that very moment was to use his eyes and make him describe whatever he was seeing until the students decided that they weren't that interested anymore and made their way back to their dorm.

"What is it?" Eiko quickly asked, not wanting to be left out.

At first there was no response. The girl repeated her question louder, assuming that all the whispers around had muted her words. When there was no response again, though, she felt a cold shiver run down her spine. Eiko tugged on sleeve of Dexter's shirt in a vain attempt to get his attention.

"You don't want to know." Dexter trailed off. His words were shaky as he backed away from the crowd, pulling Eiko along with him.

The girl was taken by surprise by the sudden action and almost fell over still clutching his sleeve. She stumbled forwards and when she bumped into him, he managed to hold her balance. "Dexter, wait!" She whined, however the boy did not listen. He was adamant on taking them as far away as he could. When they got to the front gate of the school, Eiko dug her heels into the ground and used all her strength to pull the boy backwards. The lingering snow made it hard to walk and the chilly air made the girl's cheeks and nose redden. She didn't care about the awful weather, though – the only thing she wanted to know what was going on and yet her best friend was keeping it a secret from her.

"Tell me, Dexter," Eiko mumbled out, glaring into his back that was facing her. The boy's shoulders were slouched in despair and his eyes were set on the ground.

There was heavy silence that followed. Eiko did not know whether minutes or hours had passed before the boy finally turned to her. His features were twisted in sadness and he looked like he was in a mental battle with himself. It was weird seeing Dexter so weak and vulnerable, though that made Eiko want to help him even more. When the boy opened his mouth to speak, however, no words came out at first. He stopped for a moment and took a deep breath in order to calm his raging nerves.

"It's Christian…" He trailed off, glancing away in shame. "He's… He's dead."

Eiko's blood ran cold.

Her eyes widened in surprise and she felt like all air had left her lungs. The statement was a punch in the gut and her mind had a hard time processing the information. She was suddenly more aware of the coldness surrounding them. There were cold beads of sweat starting to form across her forehead that could only be rivaled by the tiny snowflakes falling from the sky. It had started snowing again, although the girl did not notice at first – she had gone into a trance. Countless memories were flooding through her mind, making it impossible for her to function normally again. She felt sick to her stomach and wanted to puke, and her body stood completely still like a mannequin as if she was frozen in time.

Christian was dead.

All the warning signs turned out to be true. What Eiko had first thought to be a small problem that she could fix, now seemed to be something much bigger, something she had no clue about. The realization that her efforts had been in vain ever since the beginning hit her and she almost fell forward. Her knees were shaking and she felt extremely weak. It was like her body was going into shock – the panic flooding through her veins made the processes in her body slow down. That wasn't right. Even if St Ambrose was a creepy school with plenty of suspicious secrets, they wouldn't kill one of their own students. It didn't make any sense because they wouldn't be able to get away with it. Despite not knowing the reason for the boy's death, Eiko was sure that it couldn't have been anyone from the school. There was no way…

"Eiko?"

Dexter's voice was faint in the distance, muted by the many thoughts and memories.

"Eiko, come on."

She couldn't move. She was trapped in her own mind and sunk to her knees, tightly clutching the jacket around her chest in order to fight off the physical pain flooding through her body, born from the powerful emotions of agony and despair.

"Eiko, please!"

Suddenly, she felt two strong hands grasping her shoulders and lightly shaking her. When she opened her eyes, she saw Dexter kneeling in front of her. He looked like he wanted to cry but was holding his emotions in order to look strong. Eiko, on the other hand, had hot tears streaming down her face without even realizing it. She hiccupped and shook her head in denial.

"We need to be strong."

I can't be strong, Eiko thought, glancing away. It just wasn't fair. Nothing was fair in the forsaken school that was St Ambrose. Ever since she joined, her life had taken a turn for the worse. Nothing good ever happened and she always got in trouble for everything she did. One of the only two friends she had managed to make months after starting school was now dead and for what? What could he have possibly done that would result in a death sentence?

"Eiko, listen to me."

She glanced up. The snowfall around had become stronger, the white snowflakes covering what was melted off in the morning and giving a sense of security.

"We're the only ones who can prevent something like this from happening again."

Eiko sniffed, looking away. The tears were still falling down and her cheeks were redder than ever, however she could care less about what she looked like. She was in far too much emotional distress – she just wanted to head back to her parents.

"I'm scared," she shakily spoke, "I don't want to die."

Dexter shook his head. "No one is going to die anymore. We're going to find out what is wrong with this awful school and we're going to change it."

"No…" Eiko trailed off. "We'll—We'll end up like Christian if we do that."

"We don't know why he died," Dexter said. "It could've been anything."

The girl didn't realize she was loudly sobbing as she spoke. "Why do you think he was acting like he didn't want to help us?!" She loudly croaked, not being able to control all the emotions that made it hard to think and breathe. "He just--- He wanted to protect us. He was doing things on his own behind our backs because he—he didn't want us to get in trouble. Oh god… He died because of us, Dexter." She covered her face with her hands.

Dexter was at a loss of what to say. He slowly removed his hands from her shoulders and glanced into the distance, deep in thought. What she was saying did make sense, however… "You don't know for certain."

"Then what else could've happened?" Eiko sobbed.

The boy sighed of frustration. "We didn't know anything about him other than what he told us and he didn't really tell us *that* much. The only suspicious thing was his picture in the first yearbook, that's all. He didn't get killed because of us – there's no way."

"He's dead, Dexter, **dead**! He's not coming back ever again," Eiko whispered.

"This is why we need to be strong." Dexter slowly stood up from the ground and extending his arm towards Eiko so that she could take it. "We have to set things right for *him*."

The girl looked up to see that Dexter was now fully standing. His lips had curled into a sad smile that didn't reach his eyes and yet he continued to be strong. Eiko was no longer crying, though her eyes still stung and her face was now extremely cold. Nonetheless, she gently grabbed the hand that was being offered and pulled herself up.

"I'll make sure this school burns," Eiko threatened with coldness in her tone. "I won't stop until everyone here suffers for what they've done."

Epilogue

Winter came and went, leaving only despair and destruction in its wake. The current St Ambrose students lacked all signs of life, even bullies such as Kate and her groupies. They were all grumpy and in a state of tormented grief for days on end. They looked like they lacked sleep ever since Christian's death. That was the case for a lot of kids as well – most of them couldn't even process what had happened and they acted as if things were fine, as if their lives weren't in danger. All signs of bullying stopped from the fear of severe punishment and no one was ever late for class. Physical Education was replaced by History after the teachers noticed that the students would not partake in any sort of physical activity even after being coerced. That made everyone even more mentally exhausted. Most outdoor activities were cancelled as most of the students wanted to head back to their dorm as fast as possible after the school day ended. It was like they were all slaves to the fear born from the unknown – they all knew that St Ambrose was now extremely dangerous and even the smallest mistake could result in their death. The worst part of it all was that they couldn't call their parents. The Principal had taken all communication devices and prevented them from talking to their loved ones. A few of the teachers mysteriously disappeared and were replaced with even meaner and scarier ones and the whole process of schooling more painful than before.

Though Eiko and Dexter were nodifferent than the others when it came to the sudden change of behavior, they still conspired against the school. However they were much more careful than before. It had taken Eiko months to accept the fact that Christian was gone for good – she wanted to talk to Sister Anne about it, harboring vain hope that the woman would be able to help her with her emotional turmoil, though she was nowhere to be seen. At one point Eiko gathered the courage needed to go and ask other teachers about where the caretaker was, plagued by the familiar anxious thoughts that something bad could've happened. Thankfully, her worries turned out to be in pointless because everyone told her that the woman had taken a 'small' break and would be soon.

This left Dexter as the only person who was able to comfort Eiko with her grief even if she didn't want to make him feel even worse by having him sacrifice his own time in making her feel better considering he was most likely feeling the same way about the situation. Even if he wasn't that close to Christian and was in fact one of his main targets when it came to bullying, he had still worked together with him. All the memories the trio spent together were impossible to erase and even if they tried to occupy their minds with doing homework and focusing on their studies, they found it hard to maintain attention for long periods of time.

Despite calming down as the months went on, Eiko's depression only became stronger as the days passed. She started closing up when it came to sharing what she was feeling with Dexter, which in turn made him even more worried about her safety. He didn't want her to do anything stupid or rash that would get her in trouble – he couldn't afford to lose her no matter what, though that did not mean he knew what he needed to do in order to help Eiko. The only thing he *could* do at that point was to be there for her in case she decided she wanted to talk to him about her problems.

The boy was becoming more and more frustrated, though the negative emotion wasn't aimed at Eiko – it was aimed at the school itself. It was now obvious to him that the Principal wanted to destroy all positive emotions and make them mindless slaves who were controlled by fear and couldn't think on their own. Even if they both were mere students who had fallen victim to the Principal's wishes, he still believed that they were the ones who would be able to set things right. After hearing Eiko talk about wanting to meet with the caretaker, Dexter did his best to snoop around in search of the woman who seemed to be hiding from the students, however she had shared information regarding her current location with the librarian who seemed to have taken a liking towards the boy which he used for his gain.

"Hey, Eiko." Dexter waved at the girl sitting on the bench in front of one of the dorms. She seemed to be spacing out, glancing into the distance and didn't even see the boy at first. It wasn't until he got closer to her that she snapped out of her thoughts. A light blush of embarrassment spread across her features due to her lack of attention and she gave him a sheepish smile.

"Hey," she politely replied. Despite smiling, she had bags underneath her red eyes. She had lost a little bit of weight, though she still took care of herself as much as she could – she didn't want to lose all grip on life, however that had turned out to be almost impossible. It was a good thing she had Dexter, at least.

"I've brought someone you wanted to see again," he said.

Eiko's stomach dropped in anxiety. The first thought that ran through her head was of Christian, however she knew that she'd only get disappointed hoping for something that would never happen. It had been a few months since his death and yet she kept thinking of him far too often. When she glanced behind Dexter, though, she saw someone else entirely. In fact, she suddenly felt a surge of happiness flow through her.

It was Sister Anne!

Eiko excitedly stood up from the bench and walked up to the caretaker, giving her a hug. The woman looked a bit better than before, though her skin was still pale and her arms were bony when she returned the affectionate gesture. The girl let out a breathless chuckle after she finally moved away and looked up at the woman with a wide smile of happiness spread across her features.

"Sister Anne!" She exclaimed, then took a deep breath to gather her emotions. She slowly let it out and when she spoke again, her voice wasn't as high-pitched as before. "It's been so long. I was so worried something could've happened… I'm just glad you're okay."

"As okay as one can be at this very moment," Sister Anne gently spoke as she motioned the pair to follow her back to the bench. When they all sat together, she turned to them with a serious expression – it showed motivation hidden behind worry. "I know that we have been all coping differently after the… incident. However, I feel it is the right thing to let you know what Christian told me a day before his punishment."

Eiko could feel invisible tears start to prickle in the corner of her burning eyes, though nothing came out. She had already spent countless nights crying herself to sleep, fighting with her own mind for some peace and quiet. Her body was exhausted and it gave no sign of remorse, unlike her brain that kept torturing her over and over again. When she felt Dexter's hand on her own, she perked up and gave him a nod to confirm that she was indeed listening to what Sister Anne was about to say.

The woman looked reluctant. It was as if she was fighting with herself whether she should truthfully speak or keep it to herself. It was far too late to back down at that point, though, which is why she decided to let Eiko know what had transpired. "Christian knew beforehand that he was going to get punished. The reasoning for that, though is... It's hard to explain." She trailed off, thinking of the right words to say. "Do you remember when you got in trouble in the library?"

Eiko's eyes widened in surprise. "Yeah, but what does that have to do with anything?"

"Well..." Sister Anne looked at her. "You were supposed to be brought to the Principal in order to be given a first 'strike'. Christian took the blame because he wanted to protect you but that meant that he had to receive his third strike which was a death penalty. I'm sorry."

The girl gulped. Her throat was tight and she felt the same way she had in the day of the boy's death. Her face had completely paled in anxiety and she had a hard time speaking. "Oh..." She shakily replied, glancing at the ground with wide eyes. She could no longer feel Dexter's hand on her own, nor could she feel the bright and warm weather outside. Once again, she was trapped in the prison that was her own mind.

"Please, don't beat yourself up about it. It was his choice – he knew what would happen. You've done nothing wrong. You're the perfect student," Sister Anne said.

Unfortunately for her, though, Eiko did not believe her words. She had spent weeks upon weeks trying to fight against the negative thoughts that shouted in her head, telling her that she was the sole reason Christian was gone forever. Just as she had finally started to calm down and not feel guilty and anxious all the time... Eiko did not realize she was crying. She did not think that there were any tears left for her to cry and yet there she was, mindlessly staring *through* the ground as she let the tears freely fall from her face.

"Why would you even tell her something like

that?!" Dexter loudly shouted. When he turned to look at the woman, however, she had her back faced to him.

Sister Anne stood silent for a moment. After a few seconds, she turned her neck to the side so that she could look down on the duo and smiled.

"Welcome to St Ambrose."

To be continued...

ABOUT THE AUTHOR

Steve Wollett is a producer/director who has been involved in more than one hundred and fifty film and television productions that you never heard of. He directed the film, *And Now a Word from a Gamer*, a documentary about tabletop games. His show, *Behind the Curtain*, interviews celebrities and explores the real people behind the scenes.

He has published five books and is the creator of Nerd Rage News. Steve has been a firefighter, soldier, criminal, land surveyor, government contractor, health care consultant, EMT, politician, entrepreneur, and ultimately an all around nerd.

You can learn more about Steve at:

www.nerdragenews.com

Social Media Links

IMDb: www.imdb.com/name/nm5982013

Twitter: www.twitter.com/stevewollett

Instagram: www.instagram.com/stevewollett

Instagram: www.instagram.com/nerdragenews

Facebook: www.facebook.com/nerdragenews

Proof

28255789R00174

Made in the USA
Columbia, SC
07 October 2018